I0648063

Nelson Sizer, P. L Buell

The Poet Soldier

A Memoir of the Worth, Talent and Patriotism of Joseph Kent Gibbons

Nelson Sizer, P. L Buell

The Poet Soldier
A Memoir of the Worth, Talent and Patriotism of Joseph Kent Gibbons

ISBN/EAN: 9783337088224

Printed in Europe, USA, Canada, Australia, Japan

Cover: Foto ©Raphael Reischuk / pixelio.de

More available books at **www.hansebooks.com**

THE POET SOLDIER

A Memoir

OF

THE WORTH, TALENT AND PATRIOTISM

OF

JOSEPH KENT GIBBONS,

WHO FELL IN THE SERVICE OF HIS COUNTRY DURING THE GREAT REBELLION.

BY P. L. BUELL.

WITH AN INTRODUCTION BY NELSON SIZER.

New York:

SAMUEL R. WELLS, PUBLISHER,

No. 389 BROADWAY.

1868.

TO THE

Rank and File of the Union Army,

WHO

BORE THE BRUNT OF EVERY BATTLE,

RENDERING EMINENT BUT UNDISTINGUISHED SERVICES, BRAVEL
SUFFERING FROM WOUNDS OR PATIENTLY ENDURING HUNGER,
INSULT AND CRUELTY IN LOATHSOME REBEL-PRISONS;
OR WASTING AND DYING IN HOSPITALS, THUS
GIVING THEIR PRECIOUS LIVES THAT
THE NATION MIGHT LIVE,

THIS AFFECTIONATE TRIBUTE

TO ONE OF THEIR NUMBER, IS GRATEFULLY INSCRIBED,

BY THEIR FRIEND,

THE AUTHOR.

CONTENTS.

INTRODUCTION.

THE Great American Conflict condensed the history of ages into four years. Its history will never be written, never fully understood. Here and there some splendid name evinced its power and won immortality; but every regiment, every company, had its hero. There were marching in the ranks of the great army of the Republic men of genius and of culture. In a single company there might be found men who could build and run a locomotive, who could edit a newspaper, teach a department in college, manage a commercial establishment, or conduct a cause successfully in a court. When patriotism inspires a people, and a holy cause calls them forth as in this great conflict, it is not the idle, the thriftless and dissolute, mainly, who make up the ranks of the army; nor are they, as in old monarchies, the unwilling conscripts torn from family and from business to fight for a king and for a cause they may detest; but when the Stars and Stripes were assailed, when the nation's life was put in jeopardy by such a rebellion as finds no parallel in history, from the broad North every church and school-house sent its representative, every family gave up a member—

some, half a dozen each—inspired by patriotism and aroused
to valor by the dearest interests that stir the human heart.
Whenever one of those brave patriots fell in battle, not permitted to live to see the victory which his hope predicted,
it always gave us sadness. For we regard him as blest
above measure, who, entering such a contest, for such a
cause, is permitted, though maimed and crippled, to
live to see the ensign of freedom floating again over every
fort and field which the hand of treason and rebellion had
grasped. He who through the battle-shock may strive and
suffer, if he may but live to see the consummation of his
wishes, is remunerated for every sacrifice made in the tri-
umphant, holy cause. How many of those brave-hearted
men pined in prisons, wasted in camps, or fell on the bloody
field before victory was even sure! For such, and their
memory, let us shed a tear. The "Poet Soldier," whose
memoirs are preserved to his relatives and the few precious
friends who were permitted to know him during his brief
career, was among the number who, by faith, saw the fru-
ition of their hopes, but, like the faithful Israelite who expected to reach the Promised Land, fell in the wilderness.
It is a precious legacy for so young a man to leave to his
relatives and fellow-citizens, that he had the clearness of
perception to see the end from the beginning; to see the
glorious results of his sacrifices and his efforts; to anticipate
that which time only was required to reveal; and thus, seeing with gratitude the result, close his eyes peacefully and
enter upon his reward. Though his years were few, his

noble life was not brief. Experience laid the foundation and faith filled up the picture; and he, therefore, died as ripely as many a man of fourscore years. The death of such a one is a public loss, but his example and his precept shall bless the world more than many a long life.

When it is remembered that nearly every school district from which the great Union army was drawn has its hero and its martyr, many a mother who reads the story of the "Poet Soldier" will see in it mirrored the qualities of her own beloved who gave himself that the nation might live.

NELSON SIZER.

New York, *Sept.*, 1868.

THE POET SOLDIER.

JOSEPH KENT GIBBONS was born at Granville, Mass., September 9, 1840. He was one of a family of twelve children, two of whom died in infancy, and seven between the ages of seventeen and twenty-seven. His father, James H. Gibbons was a man of strong mind and sound judgment; but from early life did not enjoy robust health. He had a strong desire to obtain an education; and with the advantages afforded him at the common school, he qualified himself for a teacher, and was successful in that vocation. Knowing the value of learning, he gave his children all the opportunities to obtain it which his circumstances would permit.

His mother's maiden name was Philura Gibbons. She was a woman of more than ordinary talents; and remarkably fond, from childhood, of the beautiful in nature and art. Her father was a farmer of moderate means, and could not give his daughters the advantages of an education beyond that which could be acquired in the common schools of New England. In these schools she made commendable improvement in knowledge, and gained a superior education, considering the opportunities she possessed for acquiring it. Her father objected to her having equal advantages at school with his other children, because she could get her lessons at home without a teacher.

She was remarkably fond of poetry and eloquence; and her recitations, from the writings of distinguished poets and orators, at school examinations, elicited the warm commendation of such a man as Rev. Timothy M. Cooley, D.D., who,

1*

for half a century, was a kind of godfather, superintendent and visitor of the common schools of his parish in East Granville. She taught school several terms with admirable success; and only left a calling that she loved and honored, to assume the most responsible of all positions a woman can hold; namely, that of wife and mother.

It has been said, that "the poet is born, not made;" and the subject of this sketch inherited from his mother that native poetic talent which entitles him to an elevated place on Mount Parnassus. His talent for poetry was born in him, and he wrote, not for the purpose of gaining the applause of his fellows, but from an inspiration or mental necessity laid upon him.

His birth-place was on the eastern slope of the Green Mountain range, commanding a view of that part of the valley of the Connecticut River lying between the cities of Hartford, Conn., and Springfield, Mass. The view from this elevated place is exceedingly beautiful, and well calculated to excite the imagination of one whose mind was delighted with the beauties of nature as seen in the variegated landscape.

His father was a tiller of the soil; but notwithstanding the necessity that his children should labor for their support, he gave them all the encouragement and aid in his power to acquire an education. Joseph, though taught to perform the usual duties on a farm, never took delight in them. At an early age, when engaged in work that did not require mental action, his thoughts would revel in the realms of science and philosophy, and he would forget that he was toiling with his hands in the field. He always intended to be faithful in the performance of the duties assigned him on the farm; but his habit of imagination, thought or absence of mind, would sometimes cause him to leave the "bars down" which separated the cattle from the corn-field; and a damaged crop was the consequence. When reprimanded for the neglect, he would regret the error, and excuse himself by saying, that he forgot to do his duty, because his mind was engaged in reflecting upon a passage he had recently been reading in one of Shakspeare's plays. With a mind thus constituted, it became evident to his father that he never would excel in the occupation of a farmer; and he encouraged him to qualify himself for teaching. After having attended fifteen terms at the common school in his native district (commencing at the age of four years), he, in the winter of 1856–57, being then sixteen, attended a select school at Granville Corners, taught by Martin Tinker Gibbons. At this school he was noticed for diligence in his studies, a quiet, unobtrusive deportment, and an ardent desire to improve his mind. At the close of the winter term he resumed his labor on the farm, and continued it through the summer. He commenced a private diary, February 27, 1856, and continued it till December 8, 1862. This led him to put his thoughts on paper with readiness, and was the secret of his ability in writing for the press. The following passage in his diary of April 27, 1857, shows his love of the beautiful:

"About three o'clock in the afternoon, at the closing of a rain-storm, there was seen a rainbow; which I consider one of the most beautiful, soul-enlivening sights ever presented by Nature to mortals while shrouded in this form of clay."

In the month of May, in the same year, he wrote:

"This is a pleasant and beautiful evening. The moon is now shedding her silvery beams upon earth, and bringing to light many objects which otherwise must have been shrouded in night's gathering gloom. It is sweet and elevating to sit and muse upon the beauties of such an evening; and, I think, as did a certain writer, that there is more to be learned from nature than from books, because books are liable to mistakes, and often lead the inquirer after truth astray; but nature, if interrogated by the enlightened and truly refined individual,

'Leads in willing chains the wondering soul along,'

until it has arrived at some great and important truth. I think few have greater respect for books than myself; still, they have their origin in, and their foundation upon, the laws of nature. I say this of the scientific and philosophical works which have been written from time to time; and I say it, not because I love books less, but nature more."

On the following fourth of July he showed his love of books, as he states in his diary, by purchasing Milton's "Paradise Lost," together with the poems of Pindar and Anacreon. On the 12th of the same month he says:

"I have been reading 'Paradise Lost,' which more than fills my expectations, and as far as grandeur and sublimity are concerned, far surpasses any work I ever read."

He spent the summer of 1857 in labor and reading, and attended the Select School at Granville Corners the succeeding winter, under the same teacher as the year previous. In the winter of 1858-9, he attended a select school in East Hartland, Ct., and had for his instructor Rev. Mr. Hall, the Congregational clergyman of that place. From the tone of his diary during the term he spent at this school, it appears that he was well pleased with his teacher and the course of study that he pursued. He wrote several essays for a paper called *The Acorn*, conducted by the members of the school, which exhibited originality of thought and a vivid imagination. At the close of the term, February 18, 1859, he made the following entry in his diary:

"Think, on the whole, that I have made very good progress in my studies the past winter—have been through with astronomy and rhetoric, both of which were new to me, and commenced to read Latin."

He left school for home, and to labor on his father's farm during the spring and summer; but he did not lay aside his books or relinquish his studies. Every moment not devoted to labor, innocent amusement, or social inter views with relatives and friends, was improved in reading and study. In this manner he continued to improve his mind while he was engaged in tilling the soil. Only a few days after the close of the school, he made record in his diary of visiting the bookstore nearest to his home, which was eleven miles distant, in the town of Westfield, Mass., and of purchasing Young's "Night Thoughts." The day after he purchased this book he wrote: "Passed the day in study and doing chores." On the 15th of March he wrote: "The day has been rainy, and my time was passed princi- pally in reading Blair's 'Lectures on Rhetoric.'" A short time after this, he said: "Rain fell from morning till night without intermission; consequently, I spent the day in the perusal of some of my favorite authors." He was a diligent student of the Bible, and generally attended religious ser- vices. Sunday, April 3, 1859, he wrote: "Weather stormy; did not attend church; passed the day at home in the perusal of the Scriptures." He had a retentive memory, and re- flected much on what he read. He also had the faculty of just criticism. On Friday, April 22, 1859, he wrote as follows:

"Finished my first perusal of "Night Thoughts," with which work I have been agreeably entertained. It contains many original and startling proofs of the immortality of the soul; some sublime passages; a good many beautiful met- aphors, and one simile, in Night 544, that would do honor to any poet."

Soon after this he took up Burns' poems, and on Saturday, June 3, 1859, the following occurs in his diary:

"Finished reading the poetical works of Burns, and, on the whole, have been highly delighted with them. My slight knowledge of the Scottish dialect, in which nearly half of the poems are written, doubtless deters me from perceiving many of the beauties of this world-famed poet. I have received more pleasure from reading 'The Cotter's

Saturday Night,' which I consider this author's masterpiece, than from any other poem, of its length, I ever read."

Shakspeare was his favorite author, still he took time to read the writings of poets of less fame. On Sunday, August 14, 1859, he made an entry in his diary as follows:

"Finished reading Pollok's 'Course of Time,' which, on the whole, I like very well. Many parts of the work failed to make a very favorable impression upon my mind at the first perusal. Indeed, I have little doubt that this would be the case if I were to read it often. I think the fifth and seventh books better than the rest. They contain the most beautiful and sublime passages to be found in the work, together with some vivid descriptions and ennobling sentiments."

He seemed, at this early age, to appreciate scientific truth as well as poetry and imaginative writings. The following passage from his diary of August 24, 1859, contains some hints to scientific writers and lecturers, to which they would do well to give heed:

"Have read a few copies of the *Daily Republican*, which contain the theories of the American Scientific Association which assembled in Springfield a short time since to discuss their favorite topics. Some of their facts and conclusions are quite entertaining and appear plausible, but my ignorance of the subjects they treat upon, together with their frequent use of technical terms, of which they seem unusually fond, deters me from fully appreciating many of their theories, which otherwise, doubtless, would be both instructive and entertaining."

He had no taste for cruel sports, as will be seen from the following extract from his diary of November 23, 1859:

"Went to a hen and turkey shoot, which is the first amusement of the kind that I ever attended, and it is likely that it will be the last, as it failed to leave a pleasing impression on my mind."

These extracts from his diary during the spring, summer and autumn of 1859, are given to show how he improved his time during the long school recess, and we shall close them by giving his views of Byron as penned by him, December 3d:

"I have read nearly all of Byron's poems, and have been fascinated with them. I consider Byron second to no modern poet but Shakspeare, and 'Childe Harold' the most sublime, and 'The Bride of Abydos' the most beautiful, of his poems."

During the winter of 1859–60, he attended a select school at Granville Corners, Mass., and had for instructor Mr. Griffin. During the term, he manifested his usual zeal in the prosecution of his studies, and made commendable progress.

The following summer he spent on the farm, and nothing of special interest occurred. His mind was continually at work while his hands were engaged in toil, and his leisure moments were improved, as they had been in previous years, in reading and study.

In the autumn of 1860, he engaged to teach a school in one of the districts in Granville, but circumstances over which he had no control induced him to relinquish the undertaking; and during the winter of 1860–61, he attended a select school at Granville Corners, and had for teacher Mr. M. B. Whitney. As he was now in his twentieth year, he naturally enough looked forward to some occupation which would be congenial to his taste. He had a strong desire to avail himself of the advantages of a collegiate course of study, but after due deliberation he abandoned the idea, and concluded, wisely, to enter a printing-office, where a necessity would be laid upon him to exercise his mental powers, and an opportunity given him to improve his talent for writing, by the stimulating process of putting his thoughts in print in the pages of a public journal.

In accordance with this decision, he entered the office of the Westfield *News Letter* in April, 1861. His object was to prepare himself to edit a paper; and he deemed it judicious to learn the art of type-setting. His habits of accuracy, in whatever business he attempted to perform, enabled him in a short time to set a column of matter with less typographical errors than most compositors who had served an apprenticeship of three years at the business. He had been in the office but a few days, when our nation was thrilled with excitement by the news that Fort Sumter, which was commanded by the gallant Anderson, had been bombarded by the secessionists, under Beauregard, and had surrendered to the usurpers. This occurrence inaugurated the era of civil war in our nation, and fired the minds of all patriots with enthusiasm for the Union and for Freedom. Mr. Gibbons at once engaged in the Union cause, and, at first, thought only of using his pen for the upholding of the supremacy of the Government. His patriotic spirit was animated by the crisis, and he wrote the following lines, which were published in the Evening Daily *Bulletin*, issued at the *News Letter* office, on the 27th of April, 1861:

LIBERTY SONG.

"God save our Union!" let us sing;
And while our notes spontaneous ring,
Let each their choicest offering bring
    To Freedom's holy altar!
Our Stars and Stripes are overshaded;
How have their former glories faded!
Our very hearth-stones are invaded!
    Then rise and never falter!
Shall rebel hordes of reckless traitors,
Our "Southern Arnold's" imitators,
Of fiendish broils the foul creators,
    Infringe our sacred right?

No! Union, Justice, Liberty,
Our watchword evermore shall be;
Then let us make our Nation free,
Or fall in Freedom's fight!

Our poet was modest and unassuming, as is usually the case with true genius; and not having arrived at majority, adopted the signature, "By a Minor," for his first poetic effusions that appeared in print. He wrote only when his mind seemed to be under the influence of an unseen agency, and then words came to him unbidden. On the 5th of June, after there had been a season of flag-raising in Westfield, as there had also been through all the loyal States, the following, from his pen, appeared in the *News Letter:*

THE FLAG OF OUR UNION.

Hail to the Flag that so proudly floats o'er us!
    Hallowed and loved be the land where it waves;
Still may false traitors and foes crouch before us,
    Nor wantonly trample our forefathers' graves.
            Justice and Liberty,
            Rising in dignity,
Soon shall assert o'er this nation their claim;
            Sumter and Baltimore
            Blush that our brothers' gore,
Shed in their precincts, consigns them to shame.

Then wave, thou fair Banner, on Liberty's Tree!
    Before whom the tyrants of Europe oft trembled;
Still guard thou the land of the sage and the free,
    From the foes who disdain it, with treason assembled:
            So our country again
            Shall respire from its pain,
And sing the glad conquest that rendered her free;
            And Slavery's strong band
            Shall be rent in our land,
While proud despots tremble at Heaven's just decree.

From the outbreak of the war, he was firm in the belief that it would end in the emancipation of the slaves, held in cruel bondage by the men who sought to strike, with the bold arm of war, a death-blow to free government in America. This idea is embraced in the last lines of the foregoing poem. In that early stage of the war, few supposed that the freedom of the slaves would result from the sanguinary conflict ; but his prediction, that—

> " Slavery's strong band
> Shall be rent in our land,"

has proved literally true ; and the rulers of Europe, in consequence of the triumph of freedom in America, now tremble for the perpetuity of their despotic institutions.

When quite young, Mr. Gibbons lost a beloved sister. Time could not obliterate her memory ; and in the *News Letter* of July 3, 1861, the following stanzas appeared, addressed

TO E——.

> Sweet Sister ! though long years have sped,
>   Like meteors of the night,
> Since o'er thy lone and narrow bed
>   Grim Death first claimed his right,
> Still does thy cherished mem'ry shed
>   A halo of delight.
>
> Thy fairy form's angelic air,
>   Endowed with childhood's grace,
> Is blent with all that's sweet and fair
>   Which Time can ne'er efface,
> And hovers round my heart to share
>   A lonely dwelling place.
>
> How dark and drear life's path has been,
>   Since childhood's years have flown ;
> How deeply tinged with grief the scene
>   Which Fortune made my own ;
> Till humbled by this haughty Queen,
>   I bow before her throne.
>
> But, ah ! how soon life's sorrows flee,
>   When thy loved form appears,
> Which, dear as heaven itself to me,
>   This present life endears,

And robs the dark futurity
  Of its most hideous fears.

Then let thy presence hover near,
  To glad my longing eye ;
And when this frame shall press the bier,
  My spirit soaring high
Shall, joined by thee in concert dear,
  Ascend its native sky.   BY A MINOR.

Mr. Gibbons did not confine his pen to the construction
of measured lines, but frequently wrote prose articles of
real merit. The following, which appeared in the *News
Letter* of July 17, 1861, will give the reader a pretty good
idea of the style of his prose productions :

"We have long believed that 'a wise foe is better than a
stupid friend,' according to the old Arabian proverb; but
have never seen it so fully exemplified as in the present
crisis of our national affairs, in which the mere casual
observer cannot fail to perceive that the stupid friends of
slavery have done more within the last six months by their
rash and treacherous measures to undermine their cherished
institution, than the whole concentrated force of abolition-
ists have accomplished during the past half century. Truly,

"'God works in a mysterious way,
  His wonders to perform,'

and in the present instance is employing the Southern fire-
eaters, merely as tools, to work out their own destruction
and the liberation of our sable brethren from their galling
servitude.

"For none can fail to observe that the present contest is
between freedom and slavery, government and anarchy;
and he who now hesitates to assist in quelling rebellion is
totally destitute of true patriotism; nay, more, is an acces-
sory to the most hollow-hearted treason that ever blighted
the most benighted ages of the world. No true patriot will
now stop to inquire the cause of this outbreak, it is enough

that the outbreak exists; and our business is to inquire, not how it originated, but how it can be most speedily put down. Who, for instance, on hearing that all which he possessed, together with the lives of his nearest and dearest friends, was imperiled by a conflagration, would pause to inquire how such a disaster was produced, and whether it might not have been avoided if attended to in season? Is the present crisis an affair of less moment? Most emphatically not. For not only all our possessions and lives are endangered, but the model of all earthly governments is on the verge of extinction, unless speedy and effectual measures are taken for its restoration.

"Then let us rouse ourselves to the herculean task of defending our country against its traitorous assassins, and wash the stain of slavery from our nation's honor, if need be, with the blood of the Southern rebels. Much has already been done on the part of the Government, but more still remains to be accomplished; for, although the rebels are dispossessed of many of their strongest fortifications, and becoming greatly intimidated in consequence of it, still we can never hope for a permanent peace until an entire submission is made by the rebels, and their ring-leaders are given up to the Government as a pledge of their future loyalty."

His mind dwelt much upon the future life, and the meeting of loved ones in that land where sickness and death never enter, and where partings and farewells are unknown. The last verse in the following hymn, shows that he had a foretaste of heavenly joys in the presence of the "Father of Love," and "the friends of other days." It was published July 31, 1861:

THE CHRISTIAN'S PRAYER.

Father of Love! on Thee I call
　To guide my steps in Wisdom's way;
Oh! grant that I may never fall
　Beneath Temptation's crushing sway.

But may Thy influence divine
    Dispel the storms that whelm me round—
Dark Vice to her own realm consign,
    And widen Virtue's narrow bound.

Though nameless ills have o'er me fled,
    And left their footprints on my brow,
Still Thou canst raise the drooping head
    If to Thy will it deigns to bow.

Thus shielded by Thy sov'reign power,
    My earthly pilgrimage shall seem
A foretaste of Thy heav'nly bower,
    Where bliss eternal reigns supreme.

And when death's joyful hour shall come,
    And set my uncaged spirit free ;
Oh ! waft me to Thy hallowed home,
    Beyond the storms that sweep life's sea.

There, rapt in sweet communion dear,
    With saints—the friends of other days,
This heart shall still Thy worth revere,
    These lips still murmur grateful praise.

BY A MINOR.

The sons of the Puritans were educated to observe the Sabbath day, and " keep it holy." Our poet was a lover of he Sabbath, not as a day of bodily rest merely, but as a ime to hold communion with the "Author" of this hallowed day. With this mental inspiration, it is not strange hat he should have penned the following lines, published Sept. 11, 1861 :

A SABBATH MORNING.

A cloudless morn succeeds the vanished night,
    And breathes a holy fragrance through the air ;
All nature smiles, enraptured with delight,
    And basks serenely in the sun's bright glare ;
The very trees a sacred influence share,
    And wave in adoration to their God,
Whose praise the birds in carols sweet declare ;
    While spires, at distance, mark the hallowed road
That leads to " heaven of heavens," our Sire's sublime abode.

Now, pensive Nature, draped in robes serene,
  Breathes through her hushed domains a pensive prayer
To Him who framed this heaven-inspiring scene,
  His gracious worth and goodness to declare—
Of immortality let none despair,
  Where'er we turn it glows with living fire,
And warns frail man to flee temptation's snare
  In tones as sweet as flowed from David's lyre—
  Of gifted bards of old the true poetic sire.

Who has not felt this soul-entrancing theme
  Inspire his bosom with devotion's fire ?
Whose heart not echoes the inspiring hymn,
  Rapt Nature chants to her Eternal Sire ?
Till lifted on the wings of chaste desire
  Th' enraptured spirit spurns at earthly joys,
And yearns for scenes where bliss doth ne'er expire—
  Where neither time, nor moth, nor rust destroys,
  Nor bitter poisonous dregs life's sweetest cup alloys ?

I thank thee, Author of this hallowed scene,
  That Thou has decked me in an earthly mould,
To live and suffer with the sons of men
  A few brief years, then pass to realms unknown,
Where Thy superior wisdom shall unfold
  With splendor that doth human thought excel ;
And though I may not Thy *design* behold,
  In lodging me in this terrestrial cell,
  Still will I trust in Thee, and rising doubts dispel.

The following item appeared in the *News Letter* of September 11, 1861 :

" In the present issue we publish the last of a series of poetic effusions ' By a Minor,' as the author has recently outgrown his minority, and will publish his future contributions over the signature of J. K. G."

His first contribution under his new signature, was on the 23d of October, 1861. It will be remembered that the rebel steamer, *Jeff Davis*, was lost at sea, and this occurrence called out the following appropriate stanzas :

WRECK OF THE JEFF. DAVIS

The dauntless steamer swept the tranquil deep,
  And deemed her fame uplifted to the skies ;
For winds had lulled the waves to calmest sleep,
  And conscious Nature, rapt in vague surmise,
Beheld false traitors spurn her precepts wise.
  And is it thus, O righteous Heav'n ! that they
Who grossly trample Friendship's holiest ties,
  Receive thy gracious smile's approving ray
To gild their path to shame, and shield them from dismay ?

But hark ! with frightful swell the billows rise,
  And spread a direful consternation round ;
The freighted ship heeds not men's feeble cries,
  But, plunging o'er the waves with desp'rate bound,
Reels—falls—and sinks amid the deaf'ning sound !
  The wretched thieves their boasted prize disdain,
And dream no more of conquest, laurel-crown'd ;
  Some reach the shore, some sink beneath the main,
While Nature, thrilled with joy, thus swells th' exulting strain.

"Sound the loud anthem, O Land of the Free !
  For the proud boast of tyrants lies whelmed in the sea.
Who *now* shall dare question the justice of Heaven,
  And tarnish with doubts her immutable laws ?
For awhile tho' Vice triumphs, ere long it is riven,
  And expires in the web its own treachery draws.
Exult then in triumph, and raise the glad song
To Him who has sundered the power of the strong.

"Awaken, fair Freedom's memorial band !
  And know thy proud heritage ever shall stand.
For as souls are bedimmed by the clay that encumbers,
  But flash forth to view from the door of the tomb ;
So Liberty's fire never dies, but oft slumbers,
  To awake and the hour's darkest peril relume.
Then swell the loud anthem in praise to thy Maker,
Thy country is His, and He ne'er will forsake her.

"Arouse, ye invincible sons of the brave !
  Assert the proud honor your forefathers gave :

And your sires who repose 'neath the clods of the valley,
Shall hear the sad tale of your national blight,
  And straight in the van of your legions will sally,
And marshal to victory, Truth and the Right ;
  Then on to the conflict, ye sons of the brave!
  And preserve the rich blessings your sires died to save."

J. K. O.

The doctrine that the spirits of our departed friends take cognizance of what is transpiring on earth, has been investigated by many men of sound minds of late years. The Bible is quite plain on this topic, and those who have examined the subject candidly and without prejudice, believe that the spirits of the dead have knowledge of what is transpiring on earth. The following, as well as some other poems by Mr. Gibbons, shows that this subject had not escaped his notice. It was first published Dec. 25, 1861 :

ANGEL VISITANTS.

When the day has taken its mystical flight
  To distant realms unknown,
And the mournfully-pensive, mysterious night
  Re-ascends her sable throne,
And her vassal, Sleep, that magician wild,
  Whose sway extends o'er all,
Conjures to the view of the fondly beguiled
  Their destiny's rise or fall :

Then the kindred spirits of by-gone days—
  New-robed in seraphic attire,
And illumed by the sweetly-endearing rays
  That innocence only can wear—
Descend on their missions of mercy benign
  From Heaven's enchanted bound,
To the halls where their long-severed kindred recline,
  Which their presence makes holy ground.

First, the mother that watched o'er my childhood days
  With a seraph's tender care,
And taught me in treading life's thorny maze
  To avoid temptation's snare ;

And still true to her trust as in days of yore,
   While my longing spirit thrills
To join her again on the heavenly shore,
   Thus her message of love instills :

" Still yearns my son in the spirit world
   To rejoin his kindred band,
And revel in glory our Maker unfurled—
   The chief work of His master hand ?
Await, then, His time ; and a few brief years
   Will summon you home to rest,
Where Virtue and Happiness ever endears
   Our glorified land of the blest !

" Nor murmur that life's fairest day is o'ercast
   With sombre clouds of care—
That misery's poignant and pitiless blast
   O'erwhelms the crushed soul in despair ;
For the stormy ills that enshroud life's day
   With a dark, sepulchral gloom,
Refine and temper its cumbrous clay
   For the world beyond the tomb."

Then follow in concert the household train
   With their lessons of truth sublime,
Which sink in my soul, and ever remain
   To guide it through earth's dark clime ;
For as Heaven's most distant stars may cease,
   And their light thro' long years still gleam ;
So the precepts thus taught, tho' their authors surcease,
   Through memory's portal shall stream.

J. K. G.

Up to the winter of 1862, Mr. Gibbons, though a model
of goodness and morality, as far as human judgment could
decide, had not met with that change of mind which can
only be explained by those who have realized it. The Scriptures declare it a mystery ; and our Great Teacher said :
"The wind bloweth where it listeth, and thou hearest the
sound thereof, but canst not tell whence it cometh or whither it goeth : so is every one that is born of the Spirit." He
attended public worship on the Sabbath at the Second Congregational Church in Westfield. This church was then un-

2

der the pastoral care of Rev. J. S. Bingham, who was one
of the few who believe that it is possible for every religious
society to enjoy a constant revival. For this he labored,
and, during a ministry of about six years in Westfield, was
wonderfully blessed. Mr. Gibbons was one of his converts.
In March, 1862, he wrote the following lines, which seem to
be a transcript of his feelings, after having experienced the
joys of the "new birth :"

A SIMILE.

With what a soul-reviving power,
   Fair Spring in gorgeous robes arrayed,
Descends to dress her vernal bower
   With flowers that deck each rural glade.
From long confinement Nature springs,
   Beneath the bonds of winter riven,
And wafts on adoration's wings
   Rich wreathes of incense up to heaven.

So when the light of heaven pervades
   The soul that long in darkness dwelt,
And every grosser feeling fades
   Before the throne at which it knelt—
With joy the new-born spirit glows
   To see the power of darkness riven,
And finds its "inner life" bestows
   The bliss which makes this earth a heaven.

The views of Mr. Gibbons in relation to the war, were
comprehensive, and showed that his mind had dwelt upon
the subject. We give his ideas of the "Crisis," as published
in the *News Letter* of May 7, 1862, as follows :

THE PRESENT CRISIS.

"Among the multifarious conjectures which the present
rebellion awakens in every reflecting mind, by far the most
important one, we imagine, may be expressed in the following brief interrogatory, 'Can a Free Government exist ?'
In other words, have we, as a nation, arrived at that standard of moral and intellectual excellence which will enable

us to govern ourselves, or must we acknowledge our ineffi-
ciency in this respect, and submit the reins of government
to the hands of despotic rulers? Upon the solution of this
question suspends the destiny not only of our own nation,
but of the whole civilized world. For if our great and glorious nation is doomed to the utter ruin which would inevit-
ably follow the success of this treasonous rebellion, what
foreign nation would henceforth dare to hazard the experiment of a free government for fear of a like result?

"All who are conversant with our own history must be
conscious of the fact that England sneered at our theory of
a republican form of government; and that France enabled
us to acquire and support it, not from any real sympathy
for the cause, but from purely selfish motives resulting from
her inveterate hatred to England and jealousy of its superior naval power; and both of these nations, it is highly
probable, anticipated our downfall at no very distant pe-
riod; and should their prophecy prove well founded, and
the success of this gigantic and unholy rebellion plunge us
into irretrievable ruin—

> " 'How will posterity the deed proclaim!
> Will not our own and fellow-nations sneer,
> While Scorn her finger points through many a coming year?'

"But we are persuaded, however, that better things are
in store for us. England and France *dare* not interfere in
behalf of the Southern Confederacy for fear of a rebellion
by their own subjects; while the battle-fields of Donelson,
Pea Ridge, Shiloh and New Orleans—to which future generations will proudly advert as the foot-prints of a mighty
nation struggling for human freedom—have demonstrated
the exhaustless resources of the Government, the daring in-
trepidity of our soldiers, the invincibility of a just and
righteous cause, and, above all, the strong and overruling
hand of Providence bearing and directing us on to future
happiness and prosperity. Secessionism, determined to per-

ish in the Red Sea of a just retribution rather than forego its miserable traffic in human chattels, is already tottering on the very brink of destruction, and soon to take its final plunge into utter nothingness."

On the 26th of April, 1862, New Orleans, thought to be impregnable by the rebels, fell before the prowess of the Union forces, led by Porter, Farragut and Butler. This was a fearful blow to the then waning fortunes of the leaders of the "Great Rebellion," and a fine theme for our poet. Under the inspiration which the fall of this city furnished, he wrote the following poem, which was published May 28, 1862:

FALL OF NEW ORLEANS.

In that far off Southern region
Where the woes of slaves are legion,
Where the mighty Mississippi pays its tribute to the main—
Calmly sleeps the Cresent City,
Guarded by her fierce banditti,
While the evening wide extends her heavenly pensive reign—
Starts in fright—then sleeps again.

Ah! for years the bitter wailing
Of these slaves, their griefs detailing,
Rose from thence just heaven assailing with its plaint for freedom dear;
But their masters' hearts were rigid—
Moral feelings had grown frigid,
Blighted by that institution which doth generous feelings sear,
And they still resolved to scourge them bathed in many a scalding tear,
On these terms—if not too dear.

Moments skip in dulcet measures,
Lulling "Ocean's Queen" in pleasures,
Fleeting pleasures often broken by vague sounds that zephyr bore;
Still in haughty mood she ponders,
While her buoyant fancy wanders
O'er the shivered wreck of Freedom drifting down Time's sullen shore,
Till her Sibylline predictions which she raved and gloated o'er,
Echo in this strain did pour—

"Wealth is mine and power forever;
My defences none can sever,

Though on them with vain endeavor all the banded North should pour.
　　　Freedom 'neath my hand is quailing,
　　　And my raptured sight is hailing,
At a fast-approaching epoch, Slavery's triumph on this shore."
But these baseless, vain delusions which her teeming fancy bore
　　　Vanished soon to cheer no more.

　　　Morning now with purple pinions
　　　Flitting o'er night's dark dominions,
Ushers in a scene terrific, ghastly as the Stygian shore ;
　　　For a fleet, destruction-bearing,
　　　Her confines now fastly nearing,
Led by Porter, Farragut and Butler, famed in years before—
In a well-directed torrent, deathful, fiery missiles pour,
　　　And she quailed beneath its roar.

　　　Finding combat worse than needless,
　　　And of former boasting heedless,
Low she sinks in tame submission that ne'er bowed to right before ;
　　　And her boasted consort, Cotton,
　　　(Long since buried and forgotten)
For a final expiation for his guilty reign of yore,
Pampered by an institution which Archangels e'en deplore—
　　　Winds to heaven, an offering bore.

　　　But a fearful retribution
　　　Frowning o'er this institution,
Threats to whelm its perpetrators in a flood of human gore ;
　　　And this great secession craven,
　　　Whose destruction is engraven
On the hearts and swords of those who Freedom's cause restore,
Whose brief days e'en *now* are numbered as Belshazzar's were of yore—
　　　Soon shall sink to rise no more.

　　　Heavenly Father ! mercy-loving,
　　　And in righteousness reproving,
Thou who reared fair Freedom's structure on this heaven exalted
　　　May Thy strong, right arm protect us,　　　　[shore ;
　　　And Thy light divine direct us
How in Wisdom's narrow pathway through the climes of peace to soar,
And our trampled, sable brethren to their native rights restore—
　　　Thus to praise Thee evermore !　　　　J. K. G.

Mr. Gibbons, though usually grave and somewhat taci-
turn, was not wholly devoid of a relish for the gay and

mirthful.   But his mirth never had a tendency towards vul-
garity, and his wit was of an elevated character, the ten-
ency of which was to refine, and not debase.   The following, introduction and all, from his pen, shows that he was
not wanting in true wit.   Published June 4, 1862 :

THE UPS AND DOWNS OF LIFE.

MR. EDITOR :—The following lines which have been ascribed to the
pen of Saxe—though some critics have had the incredulity to question
their authenticity—are sent you for insertion in the *News Letter*, if you
think them worthy. And whether or not Saxe originally penned them
—which is indeed a very difficult question to determine—is a subject
of minor importance ; since the merit of all literary productions de-
pends upon their own intrinsic worth, and not, as some suppose, upon
their authorship.   J. K. G.

> The morn, adorned in her gorgeous hue,
>   Dewed the earth from her life cheering cup ;
> And the sun first greeted the transient dew,
>   And then told it to "dry up :"
>
> When a man, in his own conceit grown wise,
>   Walked forth the scene to review,
> And instruct his lad in the mysteries
>   Of his sage experience true.
>
> "Thou art little versed, my lad," said he,
>   "In the ups and downs of life ;
> Then listen while I relate to thee,
>   A lesson with wonder rife.
>
> "On most, if not all, who inhabit this ball,
>   Does Fortune both smile and frown—
> First raises the hopes of her credulous dupes,
>   And then hurls them roughly down.
>
> "Even thus for long years, steeped in misery's tears,
>   Spurned down by her harshest decree,
> Did I plod my rough way till my locks had grown gray,
>   Through a world void of comfort for me.
>
> "But wondrous to tell ! a change now befel,
>   Through Fortune's reversed decree ;
> For one day I was run for a constable,
>   But the next, *one run for me.*

> " At last did Fortune on me gleam,
>   And 't was my chance to win ;
> For strange to you though the fact may seem,
>   The *last run I got in.*"

All true patriots desire the melioration of the human race, and the advancement of intelligence and virtue among the people of all nations. Mr. Gibbons was not only a true patriot, but a philanthropist ; and loved all mankind, as well as his country. This innate sentiment of his mind led him to hate oppression, in all its varied forms, and especially slavery, as it existed in our country. He saw the justness of the cause in which John Brown was engaged, however rash and ill-advised the means he employed to carry it out, and in July, 1862, wrote the following introduction to the John Brown song :

The following spirited lyric which originally appeared in the Kansas *Herald*, is universally acknowledged to be one of the most remarkable productions of the age ; and the enthusiasm which it awakened in the Union Army has been unbounded. It is, indeed, to the loyal Americans of the present day what the " Marseilles Hymn " was to the French patriots, and " Bruce's Address " to the Scots ; and we venture to affirm that, in the true essence of lyric poetry it is no whit inferior to either of these meritorious productions, notwithstanding the quaint *homeliness* which everywhere pervades it, and, which, if duly appreciated, will be admitted to form one of its most enduring characteristics ; as it contributes, in no small degree, towards giving it that indescribable *something*, which the literary world has always been content to denominate the highest effort of true genius without being able to point out the primary elements of which it is composed :

Old John Brown's body lies a-mouldering in the grave,
While the bondmen all are weeping whom he ventured for to save ;
But though he lost his life a-fighting for the slave,

> His soul is marching on,
>   Glory, glory, Hallelujah !
>   Glory, glory, Hallelujah !
>   Glory, glory, Hallelujah !
> His soul is marching on.

John Brown was an hero undaunted, true and brave,
And Kansas knew his valor when he fought her rights to save ;
And now, though the grass grows green above his grave,
                    His soul is marching on.

He captured Harper's Ferry with his nineteen men so few,
And frightened Old Virginia till she trembled through and through ;
They hung him for a traitor—themselves a traitor crew,
                    But his soul is marching on.

John Brown was John the Baptist of the Christ we are to see ;
Christ, who of the bondmen shall the Liberator be ;
And soon through all the South the slaves shall all be free,
                    For his soul goes marching on.

John Brown he was a soldier—a soldier of the Lord ;
John Brown he was a martyr—a martyr to the Word ;
And he made the gallows holy when he perished by the cord,
                    For his soul goes marching on.

The battle that John Brown begun, he looks from heaven to view,
On the army of the Union with its flag, red, white and blue ;
And the angels shall sing hymns o'er the deeds we mean to do,
                    As we go marching on !

Ye soldiers of Jesus, then strike it while you may,
The death-blow of Oppression in a better time and way,
For the dawn of Old John Brown is a-brightening into day,
                    And his soul is marching on,
                    Glory, glory, Hallelujah !
                    Glory, glory, Hallelujah !
                    Glory, glory, Hallelujah !
                    His soul is marching on.

The love of liberty and a republican form of government,
was never more nobly illustrated in the history of the world,
than by the eagerness and willingness with which the young
men of the free States volunteered to fight for the maintenance of the Government of the United States from its threatened overthrow by armed traitors. The sons of the wealthy,
brought up in refined society, those of clergymen, presidents
of colleges, and all kinds of professional men, as well as the
sons of farmers and mechanics, who might be at school or

laboring with their hands, alike offered themselves, and were eager to join the Union army. From the beginning of the war, Joseph K. Gibbons had a desire to enlist; but before he had arrived at his majority, his father objected to his joining the army, and that ended the matter for that time. When, however, he had arrived at lawful age, he thought his duty to his country was above everything else. He loved his father and his brothers, but his attachment to the Government that had protected him rose above that selfishness which bestows its love upon a few individuals, to the neglect of mankind.

Soon after the seven days' battles before Richmond, which ended in the repulse of the Union forces on the 4th of July, 1862, the soul of the nation was depressed. On the 1st of July, 1862, President Lincoln issued a call for 300,000 more troops. It was in response to this call that the 34th Massachusetts regiment was raised in the western part of the State. Company G of this regiment was raised in Westfield, and a number of young men, from the most influential and reputable families in the place, joined it. Mr. Gibbons seemed to feel as if a *necessity* was laid upon him to join the army, and day and night his mind dwelt upon the subject. He went from Westfield to Granville, to consult with his father relative to enlisting, and after a long talk about the hardships and privations of a soldier, and his naturally feeble constitution, it was found that arguments would avail nothing, and the father said: " Joseph, go, my son; but I I shall never see you again in this world, after you have entered the army." He returned to Westfield, went immediately to the selectmens' office and recorded his name as a volunteer; and the gloom that had rested on his face for several days vanished, and it was lifted up with a cheerful smile of hope, which the withering hand of time can never efface from our memory. He was full of life and animation, and immediately set about making preparations to go with his regiment to Camp Wool, at Worcester. His last work

2*

at the *News Letter* office, was to put in type the following acrostic:

ACROSTIC.

Since thy loved spirit left its native skies
And sought a dwelling in this world below,
Reluming with its heavenly-seeming guise
All kindred hearts with pure affection's glow,
How rare have been the joys thy charms on all bestow !

Now circling years have winged their mystic flight,
And ushered in thy life's third lustrum fair—
Oh ! may'st thou long illumine Friendship's sight ;
May guardian angels holy converse share,
In sweet communion with thy soul, to shield thee from all care !

But may thy days in joyous currents flow,
Unruffled by the stormy cares of time ;
Each passing hour diffuse a roseate glow
Like richest incense o'er thy form sublime ;
Long may'st thou thus remain the grace and glory of our clime.

J. K. G.

After having been in camp a short time, he wrote as follows: "I like it, thus far, as well as I expected. Twenty men of our company were mustered into service on Saturday afternoon. We had no religious service here on Sunday, on account of the rain."

The regiment left Camp Wool August 12, 1862, by way of Norwich, Ct., for its destination near Washington city. On the 28th of August, 1862, Mr. Gibbons wrote to us as follows:

"Our regiment arrived at Washington on the 17th of August, and marched to Camp Casey, on Arlington Heights, the next day, where we remained until the Friday following. We then marched to Alexandria, and camped out till the next Sunday, when we removed to our present encampment. Our company is in excellent spirits, and would evidently like nothing better than an opportunity to show the rebels the full extent of their power and discipline.

"Before enlisting, I had often read of the vast influence

which the famous 'John Brown song' had exerted in our army, and supposed, naturally enough, that the accounts of it were, at least, highly colored, but I have arrived at the conclusion that not one half has yet been told. One truly feels that his " soul is marching on," and can never be stayed until the last vestige of slavery shall be annihilated."

Again, under date of Camp Worcester, Va., Sept. 9, 1862, he wrote the following, which breathes the spirit of true patriotism:

" I acknowledge the receipt of several back numbers of the *News Letter*, whose contents were devoured by our company with a rapacity that would seem incredible to one who is not inured to the scarcity of literary food which a life in camp necessarily brings.

" Our regiment has not yet been called into active service, but still remains under marching orders. One company of our regiment is marched, daily, to Alexandria, to quell riots and to gather up straggling soldiers. We frequently pass the building rendered sacred to every loyal heart by the blood of the martyr Ellsworth, and hereafter to be blazoned by that divine effulgence which coming generations will delight to throw around this noble relic of American patriotism. And none, it seems to me, who are possessed of a single spark of humanity, can contemplate the untimely fate of young Ellsworth without feeling that he, too, is ready to make a similar sacrifice, if his country requires it of him.

" Many persons are disheartened at the late sudden overturn in our national affairs, caused by the late reckless raid of Jackson towards the Capital; but I have no share in this feeling, and incline to the opinion that it is the enemy's condition that is desperate instead of ours, and that this very desperation forced them into an untimely raid which will ultimately prove their ruin, and bring the present fearful contest to a happy and peaceful termination.

" Our company enjoy tolerable health. One-fourth of the

men, perhaps, are unfit for duty; but none, I believe, are dangerously sick. A young man, brother to the chaplain of our regiment, died last night of dysentery.

"I have often heard of instances of soldiers being poisoned, but place no reliance in these reports. I think that if the soldiers are permitted to live until poisoned by the people living in these parts, their days will not be shortened. For my own part, I have never hesitated to purchase of the inhabitants of any place through which I have passed, and have never been injured by so doing.

"The soldier's life is much as I expected to find it. I have never regretted that I enlisted, and think I never shall, be the result what it may."

A little after this he wrote:

"About one-fourth of our company are off from duty on account of ill-health. The regiment is now in camp near Fort Lyon, situated within half a mile of Camp Worcester."

On the 22d of Sept., 1862, President Lincoln issued his Emancipation Proclamation, giving freedom to slaves, in States and parts of States, on and after January 1, 1863. This proclamation called out Mr. Gibbons' poetical talent, and, under date of Camp Lyon, Va., Oct. 7, 1862, he wrote the following:

LINCOLN'S EMANCIPATION PROCLAMATION.

"Behold, I will send my messenger, and he shall prepare the way before me."
MALACHI iii. 1.

Uttered by Jehovah's sanction, through His Prophet's sacred pages,
  Which proclaimed the happy advent of the righteous reign of peace,
Was this soul-inspiring promise, which again these latter ages,
  In their mystic course have reproduced to bid our trials cease.
For our Nation's great redemption this eventful day presages,
  Which has seen our servile bondmen to the heights of freedom reared
By our Nation's wise Preserver, who our toil and grief assuages,
    With the knowledge that foul Treason's stain is from our country
      cleared.

Glorious message ! sent from Heaven for the healing of the nations !
  Joyous harbinger of Freedom's peaceful, pure, unsullied reign !
Whose great framer shall inherit every hero's heart's libations
  And a name that world-wide Washington might emulate in vain ;
For these words of wondrous import, though but few and plainly spoken,
  Having once been sent adrift, are doomed forever to expand ;
Till the writhing chains of bondage fall beneath their mystic token,
  And the Nation's future glory is with Freedom's rainbow spanned.

Father Abraham ! honored parent of a Heaven-protected Nation !
  Who, unaided, dared withstand the shock of Treason's direful brood,
Till thy glowing spirit kindled into wildest adoration,
  All the kindred hearts of Freedom with like fortitude imbued !
Words can never frame a tribute equal to thy deed's high merit,
  And we shrink beneath the effort all unable to resume ;
But our children's childrens' praises shall extol thy hallowed spirit,
  While they deck, with rural chaplets rare, thy ever-honored tomb.

J. K. G.

CAMP LYON, VIRGINIA, *October* 7, 1862.

VICTORY.

> " So close earth's arms around the true and brave,
>   Who follow duty but to find a grave."

Many would prefer that their hero, if he must die, should
fall on the field of battle, and should be publicly heralded
to the world in the long list of honored braves whose lives
have bought a victory. Yet the writer of this sketch thinks
differently. It is well that an opportunity should be given,
once in a while, to show the patient martyrdom of those
who have lost their lives for the great cause, through linger-
ing disease. Theirs is a glorious record. With enfeebled
bodies, they yet offered themselves gladly for the service of
their country. With weary feet they marched, looking aloft
to God and the flag they loved for strength. With aching
limbs they did not shun the exposure and danger of the
picket-watch, or the irksome duties of camp. Theirs was a
quiet, steady patriotism. It was no fire to flash out sud-

denly, and then perish as soon. Their strong souls quick-ened their weak bodies; and, while they had power to stand, they sought no rest. When at last they were compelled to keep their tents, they yet hoped against hope. In spite of all discomforts, of insufficient attendance, of careless or im-proper medical treatment, they lingered near the sound of battles in which they yearned in vain to join. Then, when at last the heart gave up, and longed eagerly for home, it was too late. Rough hands of rough soldier-nurses closed the eyes of a comrade stricken by disease, but fallen with his face to the foe.

It was pitiable in the days that preceded the admirable labors of our Christian and Sanitary Commissions to visit our ordinary hospitals. There was a lack of everything that looked, or tasted, or felt like home. Wrapped in their blankets, the soldiers lay on the ground, or on the floor, or, perhaps, in cots, supplied with rations little, if any, superior to the fare of their robust comrades. Yet they made no complaint, but calmly looked death in the face, as day by day he came nearer. Ah! it required even more heroism for this than to meet him in the maddening tumult of battle, when armed with the inspiring presence of ten thousand comrades! Let a grateful country remember this when she writes of her heroes.

About the middle or latter part of October, the disease which had threatened Mr. Gibbons fastened itself upon him in such a way as absolutely to prevent his return to active duty. Yet the will to do was as strong as ever, and his only desire seemed to be that he might resume his place in his regiment. His daily record shows how earnestly he kept this in view, while here and there it betrays the fact that sometimes he doubted whether he should ever be better. Most touchingly to those who knew and loved him best, will this fact be presented in the verses which he wrote on the 25th of this month. They foreshadow his own fate, but rise grandly above any thought of despondency. They have the ring of the death-song of the Indian warrior, chanted in the presence of his foe :

THE SOLDIER'S GRAVE.

Underneath a hillock fair,
　Where the ever-weeping willow
Chants a weird and dirge-like air,
　O'er the streamlet's rippling billow,
Freedom's martyr, freed from care,
　Slumbers on his lonely pillow.

Shrine, nor pillar's honored mound,
　Decks the Hero's silent dwelling,
Deeds of valor to unfold,
　Admiration's thought excelling ;
And his praises manifold
　From his bitter foes compelling.

Human fabrics such as these,
　Time's destroying sway soon crumbles ;
Whose fell power, by Heaven's decrees,
　Mightiest monarchies oft humbles,
And earth's proudest pageantries
　From their lofty stations tumbles.

But a more enduring praise
　Thy brave actions shall inherit ;
Which the hearts of men shall raise
　O'er thy deeds' exalted merit,
Till eternal glory's rays
　Consecrate thy hallowed spirit.

There he sleeps, from trouble free,
　Life's dark strife in peace forsaking,
Till the final reveille
　Of our new creation's waking,
Calls him with the just to be,
　Heavenly joys for aye partaking.

J. K. Q.

CAMP LYON, VIRGINIA, *October* 25, 1862.

At this time he found leisure to finish Spencer's Fairy Queen, and to write an admirable and just criticism upon it, giving Spenser the position of honor he should always hold among the pioneers of our English literature.

Yet the future is not forgotten. For on the 27th, the following entry occurs:

" Pondered over the sublime strains of Isaiah, the beautiful and lofty diction of David, the elegant and pathetic style of Jeremiah, and the condensed and comprehensive wisdom of Solomon."

Again, on November 8th, he writes:

" Read copious extracts from Spenser and the Bible. The latter work forms my library here, and one which I would not exchange for any that Christendom affords."

There was light about the dying soldier at every step through the valley of shadows. The winter winds might beat upon his canvas roof. Home and its comforts might be strangers to him. There might be few or none who would speak of holy things in his presence. But there was light within that made all serene there, and that shone out through the weary veil of his flesh to guide his steps in peace to God.

None but a quiet heart, filled with love to God and at peace with man, could have indited the following exquisite paraphrase of the 128th Psalm, written at this time. It is his master-piece; none the less admirable because, though composed in the midst of camp, and under the natural depression of a painful and incurable malady, it breathes throughout a holy spirit of calm. Such voices from the scene of strife are not often heard, and it is well to pause and remember them:

PARAPHRASE ON THE 128TH PSALM.

How blest the man that fears the Lord,
  And walks in virtue's hallowed ways ;
With plenty are his garners stored,
  And bliss supreme shall crown his days.

His wife shall flourish as the vine
  That yearly swells his fruitful store ;
And round his pleasant arbors twine
  To cheer his heart with beauty's lore.

His children at his side shall spring,
  And cheer his toil from morn till even,
Like olive plants that sweetly wing
  Their grateful tribute up to Heaven.

Thus blessed every man shall be
  That loves and fear the Lord aright ;
And he shall Zion's glory see
  In visions of serene delight.

So shall his days with peaceful flow,
  Adown Time's rapid stream descend,
Till children's children's hands bestow
  The rites that mark Life's journey's end.

This was Mr. Gibbons' last poem. Slowly and quietly from henceforth he filled out and perfected the poem of his life—a true life well spent.

Winter soon began to herald it coming, through the cold winds and dreary rains of November. The canvas walls, board floor, and blankets of the invalid, gave little protection against its attacks. But with brave heart he yet hopes, though writing daily on the pages that were not to be seen until after death, "Getting no better." On November 23d is written : "Cold and windy. Remained stupidly in tent from morning till night, being too unwell either to read or write, which has been the case for some days past."

Again, both on November 28th and 29th, he writes: " I grow weaker every day ;" and December 1st, prefixes it by the emphatic statement, " Unquestionably !"   What can the writer's words add to the simple, yet strong record : " Day after day rolls gloomily by, and nothing breaks in to relieve its dull and tedious monotony."

A ray of light breaks in for a moment in the early part of December, but only to vanish speedily.   On the fourth of that month he was told by the doctor that he should be sent North soon, and visions of home must have lightened his sad heart.   On the sixth he was transferred from his own, to the hospital quarters, where he could receive better attention ; but the change could only soothe his last few hours.

We come now to the last entry in this faithful private record of a soldier's experience.   On the 8th of December, his trembling hand has written : " Still gaining a little, I trust, but long to be getting North, even though it should prove my death-journey; for I am fully satisfied that I should live here but a short time."

So, to every dying pilgrim, wherever on the broad earth his feet may have carried him, comes the eager desire to see his home once more before his eyes are closed in death. Often it is denied, and this cross is added to the sorrows that are purifying the soul.   Only in visions of the night, only in dreams of the day, come the faces of those never to be seen again on earth; and the voices of those who directed childhood's timid steps seem to speak once again. The old home, the well-remembered hills that encircle it, the paths that once echoed daily to the prompt tread of feet that are too feeble now to trust their own strength, the forms of playmates grown to manhood but all unforgotten yet, are eloquent pleaders ; and who that is in enjoyment of the full strength of manhood can tell how bitter was the anguish with which the poor, aching heart saw this promised comfort slowly passing from its grasp?

Soon after Mr. Gibbons ceased writing further in his diary, he obtained his promised discharge from the army, and with it (but too late!) the permission to return home. Hope sprang up into strength for a moment, and the feeble body waited "for a day or two" to grow stronger, but it was only waiting for the silent, sure step of death. He shall only dream, now, as the first flakes of snow fall languidly on the plains of Virginia, of the great white seas drifted between the hills of his home in western Massachusetts, ploughed everywhere by the merry sleighers. He shall only dream in future, as the cold wind pierces his thin shelter, of the sparkling fires at home that defied the peltings and howlings of the foes without, and whose gleams suggested merry-makings and happiness in the Christmas time, and the New Year to come. Perhaps it were better so—who can tell? His Christmas feast was to be eaten with his Lord; and the New Year on which he entered was to bring him no sickness, or sorrow, or death, nor even a tear. Without end of days, and without limit of happiness, the victorious soldier was to enter into the rest provided by his victorious Captain. "Well done!" "Well done!"

A letter from a comrade written Dec. 26th, gives an account of the close of Mr. Gibbons' life. He fell asleep, quietly and peacefully, at noon of Dec. 18th; so quietly that no one dreamed his end was thus near, until he was gone. His comrade wrote: "His life while in the army has been that of a Christian," and, therefore, for him death had no terrors. For him the last step of all was from death unto life.

He had grown exceedingly weak. His brother soldier leaned over him a few minutes before his death, and asked him a question, receiving an unintelligible reply. He repeated the question, and this time the answer came: "I'm going home to-morrow." That to-morrow was already at hand, and the echoes of his friend's feet had scarcely died away, before he had indeed gone home. He did not speak again, but doubtless the unseen messengers of God were speaking to him comfortable words concerning that distant to-morrow for which we live and labor, that was now spread in awful nearness before him. Voices from that Home, voices that were sweet even on earth before Death made them immortal; voices of those dear friends of the dying man who had been called before him, mingled in the song of Moses and the Lamb that was already swelling on his ear. He heard the "well done" from the Captain of his Salvation, and at that word all the disappointments of earth faded away. For where man saw a life lost, cut down in the budding promise of its youth, before it had achieved any great deed, God took it up, rounded, orbed, and complete. When He maketh up His jewels, such lives will be found among His treasures.

Thus, at the early age of twenty-two, Joseph Kent Gibbons, patriot and poet, passed away from earth. The simple story of his life and the verses he has left behind him, are his best epitaph. Nor can any hero of this war whether he carry the musket or lead an army, have a prouder record than his—that *he did his duty.*

He sleeps quietly at his childhood's home in the village church-yard; yet, not he, but only the feeble frame that fettered a strong soul. He lives still in many a heart and home, and the works of his life survive him. And thus it came to pass, that some loving hearts gathered these memorials, and shaped them into the semblance of his beautiful life. Being dead they hoped he yet might speak.

As bread upon the waters, this little book is sent out to do its work. It may teach some hesitating heart, or make some timid soul to become of giant strength, by its record of a life of duty well performed. God speed it on its mission!

The death of Mr. Gibbons was sudden and unexpected.

Even the surgeon who attended him was not aware that he was so near the portals of another world. The following account of his last hours was given by Lieutenant Jere Horton, of Company G, 34th Massachusetts regiment:

"His health had been poor for some time, but with great courage and remarkable fortitude, he bore up under fatiguing drills and marches, and battled with colds and weaknesses. It was his aim to run clear of the 'doctor's list,' looking upon such a state of things as the 'forlorn hope.' His strong will gave out at last, and the 'forlorn hope,' or last struggle for life, must be resorted to, and he went to the camp hospital. Here he received the best care that camp life gives. He had not been there but a few days, when the surgeon called upon us for his discharge papers, which I immediately made out and delivered to him. It was not more than three days after this that, finding he was failing, we sent word to his father to come and take him home, as he would not be able to go alone. We mailed the letter on the morning of Dec. 18, 1862, and at noon, very unexpectedly, he died. It was twelve o'clock that the steward passed around, and asked him what he would have for dinner. He replied that 'he would take a little chicken and toast. The steward stepped out to get it for him, and when he returned Gibbons was gasping for his last breath!"

His body was embalmed and brought to Granville for burial. His funeral was attended at the Baptist church in that place, on Monday, January 12, 1863. The sermon was preached by Rev. Joel S. Bingham, of Westfield, Mass., who was his spiritual father. His text was: "He being dead, yet speaketh." The discourse was very impressive, and well adapted to the occasion. The church was crowded with the relatives and friends of the deceased, who came to pay their last tribute of respect to the memory of him who willingly offered his services to his country, and died a martyr to the cause of human liberty.

Mr. Gibbons, during his sojourn in Westfield, formed a friendship with Mr. H. T. Levi, a man of high literary taste and refinement. They spent many happy hours together, and their minds were in unison when conversing on the varied merits of the great authors of the past. Mr. Levi had a well-selected library, to which his young friend had access. These friends on earth are both in the "spirit world." It seems appropriate to end this little work with the following notice of the death of "The Poet Soldier," by H. T. Levi:

THE SOLDIER GRAVE.

" 'Neath a gentle hillock fair,
    Where the ever-weeping willow
Chants a weird and dirge-like air,
    O'er the streamlet's rippling billow,
Freedom's martyr, freed from care,
    Slumbers on his lonely pillow."

We extract the above stanza from a beautiful poetic effusion, written at Camp Lyon, Va., under date of Oct. 25, 1862, by Joseph K. Gibbons, then a member of Company G, 34th regiment Massachusetts volunteers. Since then our young friend has passed through severe and protracted suffering by sickness, and, finally, like the weary and way-worn traveler after a toilsome journey, has laid him down to rest. The hoarse thundering of contending armies, the fearful clash of arms and furious tread of the mighty hosts which go forth to battle, disturb him not.

" After life's fitful fever, he sleeps well."

The martyrs to the cause of liberty are not few, and among the names which will ever be held sacred and in affectionate remembrance, will be that of Joseph K. Gibbons. The golden links of that mysterious chain which serves to unite our common humanity in one universal bond of brotherhood, are not severed by death, but reach to

and within the veil which divides the known from the unknown world, uniting us still; keeping sacred and most holy
within the hidden mystic cell of memory's casket, the en-
dearing names of the "loved and lost," until we, too, are
called away, and shall have joined them in that "far-off
land," where sorrow and separation shall be known no more.

The deceased was an intimate and tried friend of the
writer of this article, and, possibly, no one knew him better
or loved him more.

Mr. Gibbons possessed a fine and well-cultivated intellect;
naturally of a desponding and reflective temperament, yet
not gloomy; truthful and trustworthy in all things; sincere
in his attachments; devoted to his country and his God:

> " The hand of the reaper
>   Takes the ears that are hoary,
> But the voice of the weeper
>   Wails manhood in glory:
> The autumn winds rushing,
>   Waft the leaves that are searest,
> But our flower was in flushing
>   When blighting was nearest.
>
> *   *   *   *   *   *   *
>
>   Like the dew on the mountain,
>   Like the foam on the river,
> Like the bubble on the fountain,
>   Thou art gone, and forever!"

Yes, he has gone! but has left in his brief and useful life
an example of Christian fortitude and pious resignation,
such as only those leave who are the chosen ones of God,
and of whom it is said, "Blessed are they that do his com-
mandments, that they may have right to the tree of life, and
may enter in through the gates into the city." His remains
have been buried in the church-yard of his native town,

where, as expressed in the significant language of his own
beautiful lines:

> " He'll sleep from trouble free,
>   Life's dark strife in peace forsaking,
>   Till the final reveille
>   Of our new creation's waking,
>   Summons with the just to be,
>   Heavenly joys for age partaking."

Sent Prepaid by Post at Prices Annexed.

A LIST OF WORKS

PUBLISHED BY

SAMUEL R. WELLS, No. 389 BROADWAY, NEW YORK.

STANDARD WORKS ON PHRENOLOGY.

American Phrenological Journal and Life Illustrated.—Devoted to Ethnology, Physiology, Phrenology, Physiognomy, Psychology, Sociology, Biography, Education, Art, Literature, with Measures to Reform, Elevate and Improve Mankind Physically, Mentally and Spiritually. Edited by S. R. WELLS. Published monthly, in quarto form, at $3 a year, or 30 cents a number. It may be termed the standard authority in all matters pertaining to Phrenology and the Science of Man. It is beautifully illustrated. See Prospectus.

Constitution of Man; Considered in Relation to External Objects. By GEORGE COMBE. The only authorized American Edition. With Twenty Engravings, and a Portrait of the Author. 12mo, 436 pp. Muslin. Price, $1 75.

The "Constitution of Man" is a work with which every teacher and every pupil should be acquainted. It contains a perfect mine of sound wisdom and enlightened philosophy; and a faithful study of its invaluable lessons would save many a promising youth from a premature grave.—*Journal of Education, Albany, N. Y.*

Defence of Phrenology; Containing an Essay on the Nature and Value of Phrenological Evidence: A Vindication of Phrenology against the Attack of its opponents, and a View of the Facts relied on by Phrenologists as proof that the Cerebellum is the seat of the reproductive instinct. By ANDREW BOARDMAN, M. D. 12mo, 222 pp. Muslin. Price, $1 50.

These Essays are a refutation of attacks on Phrenology, including "Select Discourses on the Functions of the Nervous System, in Opposition to Phrenology, Materialism and Atheism. One of the best defences of Phrenology ever written.

Education: Its Elementary Principles founded on the Nature of Man. By J. G. SPURZHEIM, M. D. With an Appendix by S. R. WELLS, containing a Description of the Temperaments, and a Brief Analysis of the Phrenological Faculties. Twelfth American Edition. 1 vol. 12mo, 334 pp. Illustrated. Price, $1 50.

It is full of sound doctrine and practical wisdom. Every page is pregnant with instruction of solemn import; and we would that it were the text-book, the great and sovereign guide, of every male and female in the country with whom rests the responsibility of rearing or educating a child.—*Boston Medical and Surgical Journal.*

Education and Self-Improvement Complete; Comprising "Physiology—Animal and Mental"—"Self-Culture and Perfection of Character," "Memory and Intellectual Improvement." One large vol. Illus. Muslin, $4.

This book comprises the whole of Mr. Fowler's series of popular works on the application of Phrenology to "Education and Self-Improvement."

Lectures on Phrenology.—By GEORGE COMBE. With Notes. An Essay on the Phrenological Mode of Investigation, and an Historical Sketch. By ANDREW BOARDMAN, M. D. 1 vol. 12mo, 391 pages. Muslin, $1 75.

These are the reported lectures on Phrenology delivered by George Combe in America in 1839, and have been approved as to their essential correctness by the author. The work includes the application of Phrenology to the present and prospective condition of the United States, and constitutes a course of Phrenological instruction.

Matrimony; Or, Phrenology and Physiology applied to the **Selection** of Congenial Companions for Life, including Directions to the Married for living together Affectionately and Happily. Thirty-Fourth Edition. Price, 50 cents.

A scientific expositor of the laws of man's social and matrimonial constitution; exposing the evils of their violation, showing what organizations and phrenological developments naturally assimilate and harmonize.

Memory and Intellectual Improvement, applied to Self-Educational and Juvenile Instruction. Twenty-Fifth Edition. 12mo. Muslin, $1 50.

This is the third and last of Mr. Fowler's series of popular works on the application of Phrenology to "Education and Self-Improvement." This volume is devoted to the education and development of the Intellect; how to cultivate the Memory; the education of the young; and embodies directions as to how we may educate OURSELVES.

Mental Science. Lectures on, according to the Philosophy of Phrenology. Delivered before the Anthropological Society of the Western Liberal Institute of Marietta, Ohio. By Rev. G. S. WEAVER. 12mo, 225 pp. Illustrated, $1 50.

This is a most valuable acquisition to phrenological literature. It is instructive and beneficial, and should be made accessible to all youth. Its philosophy is the precept of the human soul's wisdom. Its morality is obedience to all divine law, written or unwritten. Its religion is the spirit-utterings of devout and faithful love. It aims at and contemplates humanity's good—the union of the human with the divine.

Phrenology Proved, Illustrated and Applied; Embracing an analysis of the Primary Mental Powers in their Various Degrees of Development, and location of the Phrenological Organs. Presenting some new and important remarks on the Temperaments, describing the Organs in Seven Different Degrees of Development: the mental phenomena produced by their combined action, and the location of the faculties, amply illustrated. By the Brothers FOWLER. Sixty-Second Edition. Enlarged and Improved. 12mo, 492 pp. Muslin, $1 75.

Self-Culture and Perfection of Character; Including the Management of Children and Youth. 1 vol. 12mo, 312 pp. Muslin, $1 75.

This is the second work in the series of Mr. Fowler's "Education and Self-Improvement Complete." "Self-made or never made," is the motto of the work which is devoted to moral improvement, or the proper cultivation and regulation of the affections and moral sentiments.

Self-Instructor in Phrenology and Physiology. New Illustrated. With over One Hundred Engravings, together with a Chart for the Recording of Phrenological Developments, for the use of Phrenologists. By the Brothers FOWLER. Muslin, 75 cents; Paper, 50 cents.

This is intended as a text-book, and is especially adapted to phrenological examiners, to be used as a chart, and for learners, in connection with the "Phrenological Bust."

Moral Philosophy. By GEORGE COMBE. Or, the Duties of Man considered in his Individual, Domestic and Social Capacities. Reprinted from the Edinburgh Edition. With the Author's latest corrections. 1 vol. 12mo, 334 pp. Muslin, $1 75.

This work appears in the form of Lectures delivered by the Author to an association formed by the industrious classes of Edinburgh; they created at the time considerable excitement. The course consisted of twenty consecutive lectures on Moral Philosophy, and are invaluable to students of Phrenology. Lecturers on Morality and the Natural Laws of Man. Address, SAMUEL R. WELLS, No. 389 Broadway, New York.

MISCELLANEOUS WORKS ON PHRENOLOGY.

Annuals of Phrenology and Physiognomy.—By S. R. WELLS, Editor of the Phrenological Journal. One small yearly 12mo volume. For 1865, '66 '67 and '68. The four, containing over 200 illustrations, for 60 cts. For 1867, one small 12mo. vol., 58 pp. Containing many portraits and biographies of distinguished personages, together with articles on "How to Study Phrenology," "Bashfulness, Diffidence, Stammering," etc., 20 cents. For 1868, 12mo, 70 pp. Containing an elaborate article on "The Marriage of Cousins," etc., etc., 25 cents.

Charts for Recording the Various Phrenological Developments. Designed for Phrenologists. By the Brothers FOWLER. Price, only 10 cents.

Chart of Physiognomy Illustrated.—Designed for Framing, and for Lecturers. By S. R. WELLS, Author of New Physiognomy. In map Form. Printed on fine paper. A good thing for learners. Price, 25 cents.

Domestic Life, Thoughts On; Or, Marriage Vindicated and Free Love Exposed. By NELSON SIZER. 12mo, 72 pp. Paper, 25 cents.

This is a work consisting of three valuable lectures, part of an extended course delivered in the city of Washington. The favor with which they were received, and the numerous requests for their publication, resulted in the present work.

Phrenology and the Scriptures.—Showing the Harmony existing between Phrenology and the Bible. By Rev. JOHN PIERPONT. Price 25 cents.
"A full explanation of many passages of Scripture."—*New York Mirror.*

Phrenological Guide.—Designed for Students of their own Character. Twenty-Fifth Edition. Illustrated. 12mo, 54 pp. Paper, 25 cents.

Phrenological Specimens; For Societies and Private Cabinets. For Lecturers; including Casts of the Heads of most remarkable men of history. See our Descriptive Catalogue. Forty casts, not mailable, $35.

Phrenological Bust.—Showing the latest classification, and exact location of the Organs of the Brain, fully developed, designed for Learners. In this Bust, all the newly-discovered Organs are given. It is divided so as to show each individual Organ on one side; and all the groups—Social, Executive, Intellectual, and moral—properly classified, on the other side. It is now extensively used in England, Scotland and Ireland, and on the Continent of Europe, and is almost the only one in use here. There are two sizes—the largest near the size of life—is sold in Box, at $1 75. The smaller, which is not more than six inches high, and may be carried in the pocket, is only 75 cents. Not mailable.

Phrenology at Home.—How can I learn Phrenology? What books are best for me to read? Is it possible to acquire a knowledge of it without a teacher? These are questions put to us daily; and we may say in reply, that we have arranged a series of the best works, with a Bust, showing the exact location of all the Phrenological Organs, with such Illustrations and Definitions as to make the study simple and plain without the aid of a teacher. The cost for this "Student's Set," which embraces all that is requisite, is only $10. It may be sent by express, or as freight, safely boxed—not by mail—to any part of the world.

"Mirror of the Mind;" Or, Your Character from your Likeness. For particulars how to have pictures taken, inclose a prepaid envelope, directed to yourself, for answer. Address, SAMUEL R. WELLS, No. 389 Broadway, New York.

STANDARD WORK ON PHYSIOGNOMY.

New Physiognomy; Or, Signs of Character, as manifested through Temperament and External Forms, and especially in the "Human Face Divine." With more than One Thousand Illustrations. By S. R. WELLS. In three styles of binding. Price, in one 12mo volume, 768 pp., handsomely bound in muslin, $5; in heavy calf, marbled edges, $8; Turkey morocco, full gilt, $10.

This work systematizes and shows the scientific basis on which each claim rests. The "Signs of Character" are minutely elucidated, and so plainly stated as to render them available. The scope of the work is very broad, and the treatment of the subject thorough, and, so far as possible, exhaustive. Among the topics discussed are—"General Principles of Physiognomy;" "the Temperaments;" "General Forms" as Indicative of Character; "Signs of Character in the Features"—the Chin, the Lips, the Nose, the Eyes, the Cheeks, the Ears, the Neck, etc.; "The Hands and Feet;" "Signs of Character in Action,"—the Walk, the Voice, the Laugh, Shaking Hands, the Style of Dress, etc.; "Insanity;" "Idiocy;" "Effects of Climate;" "Ethnology;" "National Types;" "Physiognomy of Classes," with grouped portraits, including Divines, Orators, Statesmen, Warriors, Artists, Poets, Philosophers, Inventors, Pugilists, Surgeons, Discoverers, Actors, Musicians; "Transmitted Physiognomies;" "Love Signs;" "Grades of Intelligence;" "Comparative Physiognomy;" "Personal Improvement: or, How to be Beautiful;" "Handwriting;" "Studies from Lavater;" "Physiognomy Applied;" "Physiognomical Anecdotes," etc.

It is an Encyclopædia of biography, acquainting the reader with the career and character, in brief, of many great men and women of the past one thousand years, and of the present—such, for instance, as Aristotle, Julius Cæsar, Shakspeare, Washington, Napoleon, Franklin, Bancroft, Bryant, Longfellow, Barnes, Irving, Rosa Bonheur, Theodosia Burr, Cobden, Bright, Lawrence, Whately, Thackeray, Knox, Richelieu, Dickens, Victoria, Wesley, Carlyle, Motley, Mill, Spencer, Thompson, Alexander, etc.

APPARATUS FOR PHRENOLOGICAL LECTURES,

Phrenological Specimens, for the use of Lecturers, Societies, or for Private Cabinets. Forty Casts, not mailable. May be sent as freight. Price, $35.

These specimens were cast from living heads, and from skulls. They afford an excellent contrast, showing the organs of the brain, both large and small. Lecturers may here obtain a collection which affords the necessary means of illustration and comparison. This select cabinet is composed, in part, of the following:

John Quincy Adams, Aaron Burr, George Combe, Elihu Burritt, Col. Thomas H. Benton, Black Hawk, Henry Clay, Rev. Dr. Dodd, Thomas Addis Emmet, Clara Fisher, Dr. Gall, Rev. Sylvester Graham, M. D., Gosse, Gottfried, Harrawaukay, Joseph C. Neal, Napoleon Bonaparte, Sir Walter Scott, Voltaire, Hon. Silas Wright, Water-Brain, Idiot, etc. MASKS of Brunell, Benjamin Franklin, Haydn, etc. CASTS FROM THE SKULLS of King Robert Bruce, Patty Cannon, Carib, Tardy, Diana Waters. A Cast from the Human Brain. A Human Head, divided, showing the naked Brain on one side, and the Skull on the other, and the Phrenological Bust.

The entire list, numbering Forty of our best phrenological specimens, may be packed and sent as freight by railroad, ship, or stage, to any place desired, with perfect safety.

Human Skulls, from $5 to $10, or $15. Articulated, $25 to $60.

Human Skeletons, from $35 to $75. French Manikins, to order.

Sets of Forty India Ink Drawings, of noted Characters, suitable for Lecturers. Price, $30. On Canvass, in sets, $40.

Oil Paintings—Portraits,—can be had to order, from $5 each, upwards.

Anatomical and Physiological Plates Mounted.—WEBER's, 11 in number, $100. TRALL's, 6 in number, $30. LAMBERT's, 6 in number, $30. KELLOGG's, from the French of Bourgeoise and Jacobs. Very fine. 20 in number, $50.

For additional information, descriptive Circulars, inclose Stamps, and address S. R. WELLS, 389 Broadway, New York.

WORKS ON PHYSIOLOGY.

Food and Diet, A Treatise.—With observations on the Dietetical Regimen, suited for Disordered States of the Digestive Organs, and an account of the Dietaries of some of the Principal Metropolitan and other Establishments for Paupers, Lunatics, Criminals, Children, the Sick, etc. By JONATHAN PEREIRA, M. D., F. R. S. and L. S. Edited by CHARLES A. LEE, M. D. Octavo, 318 pp. Muslin, $1 75.

An important physiological work. Considerable pains have been taken in the preparation of tables representing the proportion of some of the chemical elements, and of the alimentary principles contained in different foods. The work is accurate and complete.

Fruits and Farinacea the Proper Food of Man.—Being an attempt to Prove by History, Anatomy, Physiology and Chemistry, that the Original, Natural and Best Diet of Man, is derived from the Vegetable Kingdom. By JOHN SMITH. With Notes and Illustrations. By R. T. TRALL, M. D. From the Second London Edition. 12mo, 314 pp. Muslin $1 75.

This is a text-book of facts and principles connected with the vegetarian question, and is a very desirable work.

Hereditary Descent : Its Laws and Facts applied to Human Improvement. Physiological. By Mr. FOWLER. 12mo, 288 pp. Muslin, $1 50.

Human Voice, The.—Its Right Management in Speaking, Reading and Debating. Including the Principles of True Eloquence, together with the Functions of the Vocal Organs, the Motion of the Letters of the Alphabet, the Cultivation of the Ear, the Disorders of the Vocal and Articulating Organs, Origin and Construction of the English Language, Proper Methods of Delivery, Remedial Effects of Reading and Speaking, etc. By the Rev. W. W. EAZALET, A. M. 12mo, 46 pp. Muslin Flex., 50 cents.

This work contains many suggestions of great value to those who desire to speak and read well. Regarding the right management of the voice as intimately connected with health, as well as one of the noblest and most useful accomplishments ; the work should be read by all.

Illustrated Family Gymnasium.—Containing the most improved methods of applying Gymnastic, Calisthenic, Kinesipathic and Vocal Exercises to the Development of the Bodily Organs, the invigoration of their functions, the preservation of Health, and the Cure of Disease and Deformities. With numerous illustrations. By R. T. TRALL, M. D. 12mo, 215 pp. Muslin, $1 75.

In this excellent work, the author has aimed to select the very best materials from all accessible sources, and to present a sufficient variety of examples to meet all the demands of human infirmity, so far as exercise is to be regarded as the remedial agency.

Management of Infancy, Physiological and Moral Treatment on the. By ANDREW COMBE, M. D. With Notes and a Supplementary Chapter. By JOHN BELL, M. D. 12mo, 307 pp. Muslin, $1 50.

This is one of the best treatises on the management of infancy extant. Few others are so well calculated to supply mothers with the kind of information which, in their circumstances, is especially needed.

Philosophy of Sacred History, Considered in Relation to Human Aliment and the Wines of Scripture. By GRAHAM. 12mo, 580 pp. Cloth, $3 50.

A work highly useful, both for study and reference, to all who are interested in the great question of Biblical History in relation to the great moral reforms, which are acknowledged as among the most prominent features of the nineteenth century. It is among the most valuable contributions to Biblical and reformatory literature.

Physiology, Animal and Mental: Applied to the Preservation and Restoration of Health of Body and Power of Mind. Sixth Edition. 12mo, 312 pp. Illustrated. Muslin, $1 50.

The title of this work indicates the character of this admirable physiological work. Its aim is to preserve and restore health of body and power of mind. The motto is, "A sound mind in a sound body."

Physiology of Digestion.—Considered with relation to the Principles of Dietetics. By ANDREW COMBE, M. D. Fellow of the Royal College of Physicians of Edinburgh. Tenth Edition. Illustrated. 18mo, 310 pp. Price, 50 cents.

The object of this work is to lay before the public a plain and intelligent description of the structure and uses of the most important organs of the body, and to show how information of this kind may be usefully applied in practical life.

Practical Family Dentist.—A Popular Treatise on the Teeth. Exhibiting the means necessary and efficient to secure their health and preservation. Also, the various errors and pernicious practices which prevail in relation to Dental Treatment. With a variety of useful Receipts for Remedial Compounds. Designed for Diseases of the Teeth and Gums. By D. C. WERNER, M. D. $1 50.

This is a work which should be in the hands of all who wish to keep their teeth in a good and healthy condition. The author treats on the subject in a practical manner.

Principles of Physiology applied to the Preservation of Health and to the Improvement of Physical and Mental Education. By ANDREW COMBE, M. D., Physician Extraordinary to the Queen of England, and Consulting Physician to the King and Queen of the Belgians. Illustrated with Wood Cuts. To which are added Notes and Observations. By Mr. FOWLER. Printed from the Seventh Edinburgh Edition. Enlarged and Improved. Octavo, 320 pp. Muslin, $1 75.

"One of the best *practical* works on Physiology extant."

Science of Human Life, Lectures on the.—By SYLVESTER GRAHAM. With a copious Index and Biographical Sketch of the Author. 12mo, 651 pp. Illustrated. Muslin, $3 50.

We have met with few treatises on the Science of Human Life, especially among those addressed to the general reader, of equal merit with this one. The subject is treated, in all its details, with uncommon ability. . . . These lectures will afford the unprofessional reader a fund of curious and useful information in relation to the organization of his frame, the laws by which it is governed, and the several causes which tend to derange the regularity of its functions, which he would find it difficult to obtain from any other source.—*Eclectic Journal of Medical Science.*

Sober and Temperate Life.—The Discourses and Letters of Louis Cornado, on a Sober and Temperate Life. With a Biography of the Author, who died at 150 years of age. By PIERO MARONCELLI, and Notes and Appendix by JOHN BURDELL. Twenty-Fifth Thousand. 16mo, 233 pp. Paper, 50 cents.

This work is a great favorite with the reading public, as evinced by the number of editions already sold. The sound principles and maxims of temperance of the "old man eloquent," are, though centuries have elapsed since his decease, still efficient in turning men to a sober and temperate life.

WORKS ON HYDROPATHY, OR WATER CURE.

Children, their Hydropathic Management in Health and Disease. **A** Descriptive and Practical Work, designed as a Guide for Families and Physicians. Illustrated with numerous cases. By JOEL SHEW, M. D. 12mo, 430 pp. $1 75.

Consumption, its Prevention and Cure by the Water Treatment. **With** advice concerning Hemorrhage from the Lungs, Coughs, Colds, Asthma, Bronchitis, and Sore Throat. Same Author. 12mo, 286 pp. Muslin, $1 50.

Hydropathic Cook Book; With Recipes for Cooking on Hygienic Principles. Containing also, a Philosophical Exposition of the Relations of Food to Health; the Chemical Elements and Proximate Constitution of Alimentary Principles; the Nutritive Properties of all kinds of Aliments; the Relative Value of Vegetable and Animal Substances; the Selection and Preservation of Dietetic Material, etc. By R. T. TRALL, M. D. 12mo, 226 pp. Muslin, $1 50.

Diseases of the Throat and Lungs, including Diphtheria, and their Proper Treatment. By R. T. TRALL, M. D. 12mo, 39 pp. Paper, 25 cents.

Domestic Practice of Hydropathy, with Fifteen Engraved Illustrations of important subjects, from Drawings by Dr. Howard Johnson, with a form of a Report for the assistance of Patients in consulting their Physician by correspondence. By EDWARD JOHNSON, M. D. 12mo, 467 pp. Muslin, $2.

Hydropathy for the People. With observations on Drugs, Diet, Water, Air, and Exercise. By WILLIAM HORSELL, of London. With Notes and Observations, by R. T. TRALL, M. D. 12mo, 246 pp. Cloth, $1 50.

Hydropathic Encyclopedia.—A System of Hydropathy and Hygiene. In One Large Octavo Volume. Embracing Outlines of Anatomy, Illustrated; Physiology of the Human Body; Hygienic Agencies, and the Preservation of Health; Dietetics and Hydropathic Cookery; Theory and Practice of Water-Treatment; Special Pathology and Hydro-Therapeutics, including the Nature, Causes, Symptoms, and Treatment of all known Diseases; Application of Hydropathy to Midwifery and the Nursery; with nearly One Thousand Pages, including a Glossary, Table of Contents, and a complete Index. Designed as a Guide to Families and Students, and a Text-Book for Physicians. With numerous Engraved Illustrations. By R. T. TRALL, M. D. Large 12mo, 961 pp. Muslin, $4 50.

In the general plan and arrangement of the work, the wants and necessities of the people have been steadily kept in view. Whilst almost every topic of interest in the departments of Anatomy, Physiology, Pathology, Hygiene and Therapeutics, is briefly presented, those of practical utility are always put prominently forward. The prevailing conceits and whims of the day and age are exposed and refuted; the theories and hypotheses upon which the popular drug-practice is predicated are controverted, and the why and wherefore of their fallacy clearly demonstrated.

It is a rich, comprehensive, and well-arranged encyclopedia.—*New York Tribune.*

Hydropathic Family Physician.—A Ready Prescriber and Hygienic Adviser. With Reference to the Nature, Causes, Prevention, and Treatment of Diseases, Accidents, and casualties of every kind. With a Glossary and copious Index. By JOEL SHEW, M. D. Illustrated with nearly Three Hundred Engravings. One large volume, intended for use in the Family. 12mo, 816 pp. Muslin, $4.

It possesses the most practical utility of any of the author's contributions to popular medicine, and is well adapted to give the reader an accurate idea of the organization and functions of the human frame.—*New York Tribune.*

Midwifery and the Diseases of Women.—A Descriptive and Practical Work. With the general management of Child-Birth, Nursery, etc. Illustrated with numerous cases of Treatment. Same Author. 12mo, 430 pp. Muslin, $1 75.

Philosophy of the Water-Cure.—A Development of the true Principles of Health and Longevity. By JOHN BALBIRNIE, M. D. Illustrated, with the Confessions and Observations of Sir EDWARD LYTTON BULWER. 12mo, 50 cents.

Practice of the Water-Cure.—With Authenticated Evidence of its Efficacy and Safety. Containing a Detailed Account of the various processes used in the Water Treatment; A Sketch of the History and Progress of the Water-Cure; well authenticated cases of Cure, etc. By JAMES WILSON, and JAMES MANBY GULLY, M. D. 12mo, 144 pp. Paper, 50 cents.

Water-Cure in Chronic Diseases; An Exposition of the Causes, Progress, and Terminations of various Chronic Diseases of the Digestive Organs, Lungs, Nerves, Limbs and Skin, and of their Treatment by Water and other Hygienic means. Illustrated with an Engraved View of the Nerves of the Lungs, Heart, Stomach and Bowels. By J. M. GULLY, M. D. 12mo, 405 pp. Muslin, $2.

Water and Vegetable Diet in Consumption, Scrofula, Cancer, Asthma, and other Chronic Diseases. By WILLIAM LAMBE, M. D. With Notes and Additions, by JOEL SHEW, M. D. 12mo, 258 pp. Muslin, $1 50.

Water-Cure Manual.—A Popular Work. Embracing Descriptions of the various modes of Bathing, the Hygienic and Curative Effects of Air, Exercise, Clothing, Occupation, Diet, Water-Drinking, etc., together with Descriptions of Diseases, and the Hydropathic means to be employed therein. Illustrated with cases of Treatment and Cure. Containing also, a fine engraving of Priessnitz. By JOEL SHEW, M. D. Tenth Thousand. Improved. 12mo, 282 pp. Muslin, $1 50.

Special List.—We have, in addition to the above, Private Medical Works and Treatises which, although not adapted to general circulation, are invaluable to those who need them. This Special List will be sent on *receipt of stamp.* Address S. R. WELLS, 389 Broadway, New York.

MISCELLANEOUS WORKS.

Æsop's Fables.—The People's Edition. Beautifully Illustrated, with nearly Sixty Engravings. 1 vol. 12mo, 72 pp. Cloth, gilt, beveled boards, $1.

It is gotten up in sumptuous style, and illustrated with great beauty of design. It will conduce to educate the eye and elevate the taste of the young to the appreciation of the highest and most perfect forms of grace and beauty.—*Mount Holly Herald.*

Chemistry, and its application to Physiology, Agriculture and Commerce. By JUSTUS LIEBIG, M. D., F. R. S., Professor of Chemistry. Edited by JOHN GARDNER, M. D. Twelfth Thousand. Octavo, 54 pp. Paper, 50 cents.

Essays on Human Rights and their Political Guarantees.—By E. P. HURLBUT, Counselor-at-Law in the City of New York—now Judge. With Notes, by GEORGE COMBE. Sixth Thousand. 1 vol. 12mo, 249 pp. Muslin, $1 50.

Fruit Culture for the Million.—A Hand-Book. Being a Guide to the Cultivation and Management of Fruit Trees. With Descriptions of the Best Varieties in the United States. Illustrated with Ninety Engravings. With an Appendix containing a variety of useful memoranda on the subject, valuable receipts, etc. By THOMAS GREGG. 12mo, 163 pp. Muslin, $1.

Gospel Among the Animals; Or, Christ with the Cattle.—By Rev. SAMUEL OSGOOD, D. D. One small 12mo vol., 24 pp. Price, 25 cents.

Home for All; Or, the Gravel Wall. A New, Cheap, and Superior Mode of Building, adapted to Rich and Poor. Showing the Superiority of this Gravel Concrete over Brick, Stone and Frame Houses; Manner of Making and Depositing it. With numerous Illustrations. 1 vol. 12mo, 192 pp. Muslin, $1 50.

"There's no place like Home." To cheapen and improve human homes, and especially to bring comfortable dwellings within the reach of the poor classes, is the object of this volume—an object of the highest practical utility to man.

How to Live: Saving and Wasting, or Domestic Economy Illustrated, by the Life of Two Families of Opposite Character, Habits and Practices, in a Pleasant Tale of Real Life, full of Useful Lessons in Housekeeping, and Hints How to Live, How to Have, How to Gain, and How to be Happy; including the Story of "A Dime a Day." By SOLON ROBINSON. 1 vol. 12mo, 343 pp. $1 50.

Life in the West; or, Stories of the Mississippi Valley. By N. C. MEEKER, Agricultural Editor of the New York *Tribune* and Reporter of Farmers' Club. 1 large 12mo. vol., on tinted paper, pp. 360, beveled boards. $2.

Movement-Cure.—An Exposition of the Swedish Movement-Cure. Embracing the History and Philosophy of this System of Medical Treatment, with Examples of Single Movements, and Directions for their Use in Various Forms of Chronic Diseases; forming a Complete Manual of Exercises, together with a Summary of the Principles of General Hygiene. By GEORGE H. TAYLOR, A. M., M. D. 1 vol. 12mo, 408 pp. Muslin, $1 75.

Natural Laws of Man.—A Philosophical Catechism. By J. G. SPURZHEIM, M. D. Sixth Edition. Enlarged and Improved. One small 16mo vol., 171 pp. Muslin, 75 cents.

George Combe, in that great work "The Constitution of Man," acknowledges that he derived his first ideas of the "Natural Laws," from Spurzheim.

An Essay on Man.—By ALEXANDER POPE. With Notes by S. R. WELLS. Beautifully Illustrated. 1 vol. 12mo, 50 pp. Cloth, gilt, beveled boards, $1.

Three Hours' School a Day.—A Talk with Parents. By WILLIAM L. CRANDAL. Intended to aid in the Emancipation of Children and Youth from School Slavery. 1 vol. 12mo, 264 pp. Muslin, $1 50.

The Christian Household.—Embracing the Christian Home, Husband, Wife, Father, Mother, Child, Brother and Sister. By Rev. G. S. WEAVER. 1 vol. 12mo, 160 pp. Muslin, $1.

This little volume is designed as a partial answer to one of the most solicitous wants of Christian families. I have for years seen and sorrowed over the absence of Christ in our households. Among the Christian people of every sect, there is a sad deficiency of Christian principle and practice at home. . . . Why is it so?—*Preface.*

Weaver's Works for the Young.—Comprising "Hopes and Helps for the Young of both Sexes," "Aims and Aids for Girls and Young Women," "Ways of Life and the Right Way and the Wrong Way." By Rev. G. S. WEAVER. One large vol. 12mo, 626 pp. Muslin, $3.

The three volumes of which this work is comprised, may also be had in separate form.

Hopes and Helps for the Young of both Sexes.—Relating to the Formation of Character, Choice of Avocation, Health, Amusement, Music, Conversation, Cultivation of Intellect, Moral Sentiment, Social Affection, Courtship and Marriage. Same Author. 1 vol. 12mo, 246 pp. Muslin, $1 50.

Aims and Aids for Girls and Young Women, on the various Duties of Life. Including, Physical, Intellectual and Moral Development, Self-Culture, Improvement, Dress, Beauty, Fashion, Employment, Education, the Home Relations, their Duties to Young Men, Marriage, Womanhood and Happiness. Same Author. 12mo, 224 pp. Muslin, $1 50.

Ways of Life, showing the Right Way and the Wrong Way. Contrasting the High Way and the Low Way; the True Way and the False Way; the Upward Way and the Downward Way; the Way of Honor and the Way of Dishonor. Same Author. 1 vol. 12mo, 157 pp. Muslin, $1.

Notes on Beauty, Vigor and Development; Or, How to Acquire Plumpness of Form, Strength of Life and Beauty of Complexion; with Rules for Diet and Bathing, and a Series of improved Physical Exercises. By WILLIAM MILO, of London. Illustrated. 12mo, 24 pp. Paper, 12 cents.

Father Matthew, the Temperance Apostle.—His Portrait, Character, and Biography. By S. R. WELLS, Editor of the Phrenological Journal. 12c.

Temperance in Congress.—Speeches delivered in the House of Representatives on the occasion of the First Meeting of the Congressional Temperance Society. One small 12mo vol. 25 cents.

A Library for Lecturers, Speakers and Others.—Every Lawyer, Clergyman, Senator, Congressman, Teacher, Debater, Student, etc., who desires to be informed and posted on the Rules and Regulations which govern Public Bodies, as well as those who desire the best books on Oratory, and the Art of Public Speaking, should provide himself with the following small and carefully selected Library:

The Indispensable Hand-Book .	. $2 25	School Day Dialogues, . .	$1 50
Oratory, Sacred and Secular .	. 1 50	Cushing's Manual of Parlia. Practice	75
The Right Word in the Right Place,	75	The Culture of the Voice and Action	1 75
The American Debater .	. 2 00	Treatise on Punctuation . .	. 1 75

One copy of each sent by Express, on receipt of $10, or by mail, post-paid, at the prices affixed. Address, SAMUEL R. WELLS, 389 Broadway, New York.

EDUCATIONAL HAND-BOOKS.

Hand-books for Home Improvement (Educational); comprising, "How to Write," "How to Talk," "How to Behave," and "How to do Business," in one large volume. Indispensable. One large 12mo vol., 647 pp. Muslin, $2 25. More than 100,000 copies of this work have been sold. A capital book for agents. These works may also be had in separate form as follows:

How to Write, A Pocket Manual of Composition and Letter-Writing. Invaluable to the Young. 1 vol. 12mo, 156 pp. Muslin, 75 cents.

How to Talk, A Pocket Manual of Conversation and Debate, with more than Five Hundred Common Mistakes in Speaking Corrected. 1 vol. 12mo, 156 pp. Muslin, 75 cents.

How to Behave, A Pocket Manual of Republican Etiquette and Guide to Correct Personal Habits, with Rules for Debating Societies and Deliberative Assemblies. 1 vol. 12mo, 149 pp. Muslin, 75 cents.

How to do Business, A Pocket Manual of Practical Affairs, and a Guide to Success in Life, with a Collection of Legal and Commercial Forms. Suitable for all. 1 vol. 12mo, 156 pp. Muslin, 75 cents.

The Right Word in the Right Place.—A New Pocket Dictionary and Reference Book. Embracing extensive Collections of Synonyms, Technical Terms, Abbreviations, Foreign Phrases. Chapters on Writing for the Press, Punctuation, Proof-Reading, and other Interesting and Valuable Information. By the Author of "How to Write," etc. 1 vol. 16mo, 214 pp. Cloth, 75 cts.

In this little volume is condensed into a small space, and made available to every writer, speaker and reader, what can be found elsewhere only by consulting heavy volumes which few private libraries contain. The collection of synonyms contained therein, is alone well worth the cost of the whole volume. It is adapted particularly to the wants of writers for the press, and those in whom the faculty of original language is deficient.

Rural Manuals, comprising "The House," "The Farm," "The Garden," and "Domestic Animals." In one large 12mo vol., 655 pp. Muslin, $2 25.

Library of Mesmerism and Psychology. Comprising the Philosophy of Mesmerism, Clairvoyance, and Mental Electricity; Fascination, or the Power of Charming; The Macrocosm, or the World of Sense; Electrical Psychology, the Doctrine of Impressions; The Science of the Soul, treated Physiologically and Philosophically. Two volumes in one. Handsome 12mo, 880 pp. Illustrated. Muslin, $4.

The Emphatic Diaglott; Or, the New Testament in Greek and English. Containing the Original Greek Text of what is commonly called The New Testament, with an Interlineary Word-for-word English Translation; a New Emphatic Version based on the Interlineary Translation, on the Readings of Eminent Critics, and on the various Readings of the Vatican Manuscript (No. 1,209 in the Vatican Library); together with Illustrative and Explanatory Foot Notes, and a copious Selection of References; to the whole of which is added a valuable Alphabetical Index. By BENJAMIN WILSON. One vol., 12mo, 884 pp. Price, $4; extra fine binding, $5. Address, SAMUEL R. WELLS, 389 Broadway, New York.

WORKS ON PHONOGRAPHY,

OR

SHORT-HAND WRITING.

Had PHONOGRAPHY been known forty years ago, it would have SAVED ME TWENTY YEARS OF HARD LABOR."—BENTON.

THE GREATEST ACCOMPLISHMENT OF THE AGE.

To any youth who may possess the art, it is capital of itself, upon which he may confidently rely for support. It leads to immediate, permanent, and respectable employment. To the professional man, and indeed to every one whose pursuits in life call upon him to record incidents and thoughts, it is one of the great labor-saving devices of the age. Mailed from this office on receipt of price.

The Complete Phonographer: Being an Inductive Exposition of Phonography, with its application to all Branches of Reporting, and affording the fullest Instruction to those who have not the assistance of an Oral Teacher; also intended as a School Book. By JAMES E. MUNSON. Price, $2 25.

Graham's Hand-Book of Standard or American Phonography.— Presenting the Principles of all Styles of the Art, commencing with the analysis of words, and proceeding to the most rapid reporting style. Price, $2 25.

Graham's First Standard Phonographic Reader.—Written in the Corresponding Style, with Key. Price, $1 75.

Graham's Second Standard Phonographic Reader.—Written in the Reporting Style. Price, $2.

Graham's Reporter's Manual.—A complete Exposition of the Reporting Style of Phonography. Price, $1 25.

Graham's Synopsis of Standard or American Phonography, printed in Pronouncing Style. Price, 50 cents.

Graham's Standard Phonographic Dictionary; Containing the Pronunciation and the best Corresponding and Reporting Outlines of many Thousand Words and Phrases. Invaluable to the Student and Practical Reporter. Price, $5.

Pitman's (Benn) Manual of Phonography.—A new and comprehensive Exposition of Phonography, with copious Illustrations and Exercises Designed for schools and private students. New edition. Price, $1 25.

Pitman's (Benn) Reporter's Companion.—A complete Guide to the Art of Verbatim Reporting, designed to follow Pittman's Manual of Phonography. Price, $1 50.

Pitman's (Benn) Phrase Book, a Vocabulary of Phraseology. $1 25.

Pitman's (Benn) Phonographic Reader.—A Progressive series of reading exercises. A useful work for every Phonographic student. Price 40 cts.

Longely's American Manual of Phonography.—Being a complete Guide to the Acquisition of Pitman's Phonetic Short-hand. Price,

The History of Short-Hand, from the system of Cicero down to the Invention of Phonography. Edited and engraved on Stone by BENN PITMAN. $1.25.

Handsome Reporting Cases for Phonographic Copy-Books. $1.

Phonographic Copy-Books.—Double or Single ruled. Price, 15 cts.

The American Phonetic Dictionary, with Pronouncing Vocabularies of Classical, Scriptural, and Geographical Names. By DANIEL S. SMALLEY. $4 50.

P. S.—WRITTEN INSTRUCTION. Should lessons of written instruction be desired, the same may be obtained through this office. Terms, for a course of six lessons, $5. Address S. R. WELLS, 389 Broadway, N. Y.

NEW PHYSIOGNOMY.

KNOW THYSELF

By S. R. Wells, 389 B'way, N. Y.

SELECTIONS FROM NEW PHYSIOGNOMY.

"O wad some power the giftie gie us,
To see oursels as ithers see us!
It wad frae mony a blunder free us,
An' foolish notion."—BURNS.

Fig. 976.—HENRY W. LONGFELLOW.   Fig. 982.—ROSA BONHEUR.

THE following selections and specimen pages from "New Physiognomy," are intended as an exposition of the general tenor of this admirable work; which has received so warm a welcome from the press all over the country. In his preface, the author says:

"We know how widely mankind differ in looks, in opinion, and in character, and it has been our study to discover the *causes* of these differences. We find them in organization. As we look, so we feel, so we act, and so we are. But we may *direct* and *control* even our *thoughts*, our *feelings*, and our *acts*, and thus, to some extent — by the aid of grace — become what we will. We can be temperate or intemperate; virtuous or vicious; hopeful or desponding; generous or selfish; believing or skeptical; prayerful or profane. We are free to choose what course we will pursue, and our bodies, our brains, and our features, readily adapt themselves, and clearly indicate the lives we lead and the characters we form.

"It has been our aim to present this subject in a practical manner, basing all our inferences on well-established principles, claiming nothing but what is clearly within the lines of probability, and illustrating, when possible, every statement. Previous authors have been carefully studied, and whatever of value could be gleaned we have systematized and incorporated, adding our own recent discoveries. For more than twenty years we have been engaged in the study of man, and in "character-reading" among the people of various races, tribes and nations, enabling us to classify the different forms of body, brain, and face, and reduce to METHOD the processes by which character may be determined. Hitherto, but partial observations have been made, and of course only partial results obtained. We look on man as a whole—made up of parts, and to be studied as a whole, *with all the parts combined.*"

Fig. 749.—A MISER.

Fig. 750.—A LIBERAL.

PHYSIOGNOMY OF INSANITY AND IDIOCY.

Fig. 434.—DESERTED.

Fig. 435.—MALICE.

THE chapters on insanity and idiocy, are two of the most interesting in the work. Not only are the symptoms and outward appearances analyzed, but Mr. Wells endeavors to trace these abnormal conditions to their sources. He treats of the varieties, the causes, the treatment, the prevention, and the physiognomical signs of insanity, illustrated amply by portraits and accounts of celebrated maniacs and idiots.

Idiocy—to which chapter twenty-one is wholly devoted—gives the causes, the education and the signs of idiocy; and is one of the best practical treatises on that subject in the language. The brain being a subject to which the author has devoted his attention for a lifetime, stamp these chapters as pre-eminently valuable and reliable.

Fig. 434, which represents a woman who became insane on account of the unfaithfulness of her lover, who deserted her, shows the lively, brilliant eyes mentioned by Dr. Laurent. She still loves; and in her mental aberration adorns her disheveled hair with flowers, and with parted lips and "hungry devouring glances" awaits the coming of her heart's idol, whom she never ceases to expect.

"Intense thought, habitual reflection, and searching inquiry of any kind cause a drawing down of the eyebrows, as shown in Chapter XIII. (p. 249). Persons who have become insane through hard study or the too close application of the mind to a particular subject will exhibit this characteristic.

"In Fig. 435 the eyes gleam with some relentless purpose of vengeance. Such a character as the one here represented is dangerous in his alienation; for he combines the cunning of the fox with the ferocity of the tiger. Fig. 436 is a woman of the Cassandra order. The eyes, abandoned to the action of the involuntary muscles (see Chapter XIII., p. 233), are

Fig. 436—RAVING.

Fig. 440.—LOVE-SICK.

rolled upward with a wild look which is indescribable. She is giving utterance to what she deems prophetic warnings of the most solemn and awful character."

ETHNOLOGY, OR TYPES OF MANKIND.

Fig. 476.—THE CAUCASIAN RACE.

ETHNOLOGY is a subject upon which has been comparatively little studied The field is a wide one for inquiry and research, and chapters on "The Races Classified," "The Caucasian, Mongolian, Malayan, American and Ethiopian Races," "National Types," "Ancient Types," are invaluable. No where else can there be found such a complete digest of the subject. In his Introduction to these chapters the author says:

"The question of race will be found to resolve itself into that of *organization*, and this determines and is indicated by *configuration*. If we desire to ascertain to what race an individual, a tribe, or a nation may belong, we must study the character of that individual, tribe, or nation through its signs in the physical system. Would we determine the status of a race or a nation, we shall find the measure of its mental power in the size and quality of its average brain, and the index of its civilization and culture in its prevailing style of face and figure.

"In so new a field of inquiry as the one which we are now entering, we can not hope to push our explorations into every part, or to investigate thoroughly every point that we may touch upon. We are, to some extent, pioneers, and as such shall do as well as we can the work assigned to us, trusting that those who follow will find their progress facilitated by our labors."

Then follows an agreeable essay on "National Types." The principal nations and tribes composed in the various races, are described in detail, with a "view to show how, in each, the common type is modified without being lost, and how, in all, configuration and character correspond."

"We shall adopt here, as best known and most generally received, though not perhaps most scientific, the classification of Blumenbach. This arrangement will serve the purposes we have in view as well as any other yet proposed, and whether it be accepted by the reader or set aside in favor of a more recent one, the value of the facts we shall here throw together will not be lessened.

Fig. 489.—THE AMERICAN RACE.

PHYSIOGNOMY OF CLASSES.

Figs. 716 to 725.

Not only does the author divide the human family into the five great races and "National types," but he sub-divides them into "classes," presenting us with groups of distinguished Divines, Pugilists, Warriors, Surgeons, Inventors, Philosophers, Statesmen, Orators, Actors, Poets, Musicians and Artists, etc. Of the poets, he says:

"One of the essential physical qualities of a poet is a susceptible mental temperament. This must be of a clear and fine—even of an exquisite—tone, to insure perfection in the art. There are all degrees of poets, from the lowest to the highest, just as there are different classes of musicians, painters, sculptors, etc.; but to excel, and to inscribe one's name on the roll of great bards, one must be not only every inch a man, but must have 'genius' as well. It has been said by an ancient author, *poeta nascitur, non fit*'—the poet is born, not made; yet we maintain that every well-organized human being should be able to write poetry, just as he should be able to make music, or invent and use tools; for has not nature given to each a like number of faculties, the same in function, and differing only in degree and combination?"

THE TWO PATHS.

The following contrasts, illustrative of the effects of a right or a wrong course of life upon an individual, are submitted to our readers. They tell their own story. In the one case we see a child, as it were, develop into true manhood; in the other, into the miserable inebriate or the raving maniac.

Fig. 761.   Fig. 762.

Two boys (figs. 761 and 762) start out in life with fair advantages and buoyant hopes. With them it remains to choose in what direction they shall steer their barks. Fig. 763 represents the first as having chosen the way of righteousness,

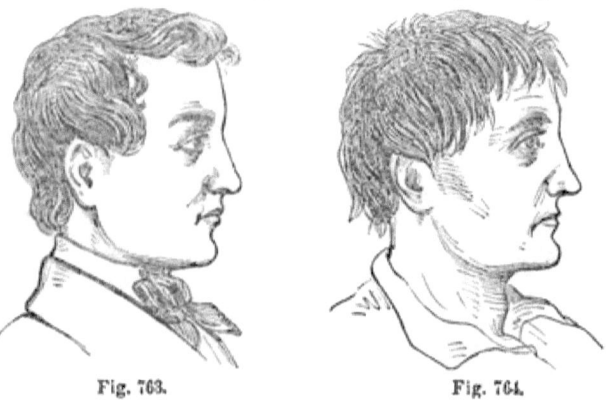

Fig. 763.   Fig. 764.

the upward path. He lives temperately, forms worthy associations, attends the Sunday-school, strives to improve his mind with useful knowledge, and is regarded in the community as a young man of excellent character and promise.

In fig. 764, on the contrary, the other boy is represented as having unwisely chosen the downward course, thinking he will enjoy himself and not submit to what he considers the strait jacket of moral discipline. He becomes coarse and

Fig. 765.   Fig. 766.

rough in feature, slovenly in his dress; he smokes and chews, drinks, gambles, attends the race-course, spends his nights at the play-house or the tavern, disregards all parental authority and admonition, and develops into the full-grown rowdy,

Fig. 767.   Fig. 768.

and as such he sets at naught all domestic ties and obligations, leaving his wife and children to beg, starve, or eke out

THE ARTIST AND THE WOMAN OF THE WORLD.

In Rosa Bonheur we see a child of inborn genius, inherited from an artist-parent, developed by necessity, and perfected by persevering exertion. From a love of them, her artistic

Fig. 982.—Rosa Bonheur.*   Fig. 983.—Theodosia Burr.†

sympathies seem to fix upon horses, cattle, sheep, etc., and if she does not take on their natures, she portrayed them on can

---

° Rosa Bonheur was born at Bordeaux, France, May 22, 1822 ; her father, Raymond Bonheur, an artist by profession, and in humble circum stances. In 1829 he removed to Paris, where he put Rosa in a boarding school. There her poverty, however, was a constant source of annoyance to her very sensitive nature, as it provoked the sneers of her wealthie school associates. On that account she did not remain long at school, but being taken home was instructed by her father in drawing. From child hood she exhibited an intuitive love of art, her inclinations tending toward the representation of domestic animals. Making these her special study, she soon excelled in their portraiture. The picture which has ob tained for Miss Bonheur a world-wide reputation is "Le Marché aux Chevaux," otherwise known as the "Horse Fair." It is now in the hand of a gentleman residing in New Jersey. Miss Bonheur at present reside in Paris, industriously pursuing her art. The great feature of her work is faithfulness to nature and boldness of design.

† Theodosia Burr Allston, the daughter and only child of Aaron Burr was born at Albany, N. Y., in 1783. Her father tenderly loved her and spared no pains in her education. It is said that "in solid and elegan accomplishments she was very far superior to the ladies of her time." She married Joseph Allston, who was in 1812 Governor of South Carolina She was lost in the schooner Patriot, on the voyage from Charleston to New York, January, 1813.

as to the life. One almost fancies he can hear her pictured casts breathe, so naturally are they drawn. Hers is a beautiful face, if somewhat masculine; it is not coarse; if strongly marked, it is still womanly. The forehead is beautifully shaped, the eyes well placed and expressive, the nose handsome, and the lips exquisite. The chin shows chaste affection, with nothing of the sensual or voluptuous; indeed, it is rarely we meet with more natural feminine attractiveness than in this artist-woman, and we dismiss her from our considerations with the happiest impressions.

There is character in the head and face of Theodosia Burr. See how high the brain is in the crown! She was emphatically her father's daughter. There is great dignity, pride, will, and sense of character indicated in her physiognomy. Nothing but religious influences could subdue such a nature. There is something voluptuous in the lip, cheek, and chin. The affections were evidently ardent and strong. Such a woman could scarcely be content in private and domestic life, but could crave a high and even stately position where her pride and love of display could be gratified. There was nothing of "your humble servant" in this person. Educated as she was, she could be lady-like and refined. Had she been uneducated, there would have been much willfulness, obstinacy, and perhaps sensuality exhibited. Analyzed, her head and face exhibit the following organs conspicuously developed—Firmness, Approbativeness, Caution, Ideality, Sublimity, Conscientiousness, Language, Agreeableness, and those of the back-head generally.

Rosa Bonheur shows a higher forehead, a more meditative disposition of mind than her associate; her head is broader in Constructiveness, Sublimity, Ideality, and the crown, and more prominent in the region of Benevolence, Veneration, and Spirituality than that of the latter. In a social point of view, Theodosia shows more ardent feeling, more intensity of emotion. The latter had more sympathy for general society, entered enthusiastically into its enjoyments; the former finds her highest enjoyment in a life of serene retirement with a limited circle of friends and at her easel.

COMPARATIVE PHYSIOGNOMY—PORTRAITS OF A LION AND MAN.

"What They Say."—Notices of the Press.

Everybody is influenced in forming opinions by what others say. And it requires everybody to know everything and to do everything. A great book, like a great public work, is, or should be, the culmination of all past knowledge in that interest. Webster's Dictionary contains the gist of all preceding dictionaries. The electric telegraph was suggested centuries ago, and all mankind, dead and living, have contributed to its establishment. So the newspaper press throughout the world may be said to echo the voice of the people. The *Philadelphia Press* says :

Mr. Wells has put the thought, the practical experience, the close observation, and the professional collection of a life-time into this important physiological work. He treats, as Lavater did, of Physiognomy, shows its harmony with Phrenology, and explains, to elucidate both sciences, the whole structure of the human body. He treats of temperaments, and contrasts the separate features of various human races, showing also how character is affected by climate. Very curious, too, are his illustrations of comparative Physiognomy, showing the animal types of the human race. The price of the work is $5.

A familiar chapter on Phrenology is introduced, and then follows one on the anatomy of the face, with a close analysis of each feature. First, the chin. No one will dispute Mr. Wells as to the infinite variety of chins; but we are sure many will be startled to hear that this unpretending terminus of the face has been quietly telling their love secrets. The jaws and teeth also tell their own tales of character. "The closest mouth can hide no secrets from the physiognomist."—*The Anti-Slavery Standard.*

The treatise of Mr. Wells, wh is admirably printed and profusely i trated, is probably the most comp hand-book upon the subject in the guage. It contains a synopsis of the tory of Physiognomy, with notices o the different systems which have been mulgated, and critical examinations of eyes, the noses, the mouths, the ears, the brows of many distinguished and n rious characters.—*New York Tribune.*

It contains a treatise on ev feature and whatever indicates peculia of character, the knowledge of which quires appropriate education to bring subjugation and be made to answer a g end, without which it would mar and jure the pleasures of life. All who afford to possess this compendium have value received for the expense.—*York Christian Intelligencer.*

It is a digest of Ethnology gives us the symptomatology of insa it treats of Physiology and Hygiene, incidentally, of Zoology. The chapter the grades of intelligence is instruct and that on comparative Physiognom exceedingly entertaining.—*American cational Monthly.*

There are very few men or men who do not, consciously or un sciously, practice Physiognomy every of their lives. They may ridicule the that the shape of a man's head, the co ration of his nose, or the appearanc his eyes, furnish any guide to an estin of his character or disposition, and yet man of business will refuse an applic employment because his glance is rest and uneasy instead of firm and decid and every lady will quietly but qui form her judgment regarding the ge man who may be presented to her at evening party.—*New York Times.*

RESEMBLANCE BETWEEN THE FOX AND MAN ILLUSTRATED.

However some may be disposed to sneer at the claims of Physiognomy to rank among sciences, the most persistent of them will guage much of his action in his intercourse with his fellow men by facial signs. That certain facial signs indicate peculiarities of character can scarcely be doubted. Mr. Wells records the result of observations of others as well as his own; does full justice, even where he differs from them, to the views of his predecessors, and with great industry and faithfulness to facts, builds up his system. He exhausts the subject and its cognate branches, and displays a masterly power of analysis and generalization. It is an important volume, and deserving of careful study.—*New York Courier.*

The work is thorough, practical, and comprehensive. All that is known on the subject is systematized, explained, illustrated, and applied. A chapter is devoted to Graphomancy, or character as revealed in handwriting. Taken as a whole, it is the most complete and reliable work on the subject we have ever examined, notwithstanding that we claim an intimate acquaintance with Lavater's work on the same subject.—*The Northwest.*

It is a voluminous and very comprehensive work, taking the student by a thousand paths to a conclusion as to its entire correctness of theory, demonstrated by multitudes of the aptest illustrations. It is very entertaining and instructive, telling the reader in little of great things he should further investigate.—*Boston Gazette.*

As far as the study of the face can be reduced to a science, Mr. Wells has succeeded beyond any other writer or delineator of character. His analysis of the different forms of faces, as indicating character, in the expression of the eyes, ears, nose, lips, mouth, head, hair, eyebrows, hands, feet, chin, neck, teeth, jaws, cheeks, skin, complexion, the laugh, the walk, the shaking of hands, dress, is fully illustrated by living and dead characters, besides numerous outlines to guide and instruct the reader. Ethnology is fully treated by illustrations of the different types of the human race, and presented in a pleasing and instructive form.—*Milledgeville (Georgia) Recorder.*

It seems quite natural to expect that the various features of our bodies should express the qualities and powers of which we are possessed. In all ages the eye has been regarded as an index to the soul, consequently it is a popular mode of expressing the qualities of another to say that such a one has the eye of an eagle, a lion, or a cat. When we think of a people of one country as distinguished by its high cheek-bones, and another by its lengthened nose, and another by its thin or thick lips, and how each country as a whole has a mental constitution corresponding to its physical development, we see reason for believing in the science of Physiognomy, and how that which is true of nations must be more or less true of individuals. Price $5, $8, or $10.—*Scottish American.*

The illustrations constitute the most essential part of a work like this. This is especially evident in the chapter on "Comparative Physiognomy," in which the resemblance between certain classes of men and corresponding animals is strikingly exhibited in the cuts.—*Methodist.*

The author properly considers Physiognomy as the outward expression of the inner man; it shows race, class, original inclinations, temperament, and also the effects of association and education. Close observation and long practice have given him accuracy in drawing conclusions from the peculiarities of the human countenance, and he has reduced his experience to a system, which is amply set forth in this volume.—*Philadelphia Times.*

Among those who have contributed to it in this country, the author of this book is honorably distinguished, and we feel pleasure in bearing testimony to the conscientiousness and ability with which he has executed the laborious task he imposed upon himself.—*N. Y. Herald.*

The principles sought to be laid down in this work are made sufficiently plain to the dullest comprehension, while they are elucidated still more clearly by the aid of over one thousand fine illustrations. The work is got up in the elegant style peculiar to this house, and we regard it as a valuable contribution to a science that as yet is but in its infancy.—*Jersey C. Times.*

"NEW PHYSIOGNOMY" TESTIMONIALS.

THE most complete hand-book of Physiognomy in the language.—*N. Y. Tribune.*

It is really a complete encyclopædia of the subject.—*N. Y. Gospel of Health.*

It will form a text-book for Physiognomists and Phrenologists; and serves to mark the progress these studies have made.—*N. Y. Herald.*

By far the best work ever written on this subject. It cannot be read without instruction and profit, and its suggestions are of great value.—*Chr. Inquirer.*

It is worthy of very high praise. To read such a kindly book, puts one in a good humor.—*New York Independent.*

Is a work of science, art and literature, whose purity of tone will commend it to all classes of readers.—*Wide World.*

All who can afford to possess this compendium, will have value received for the expense.—*N. Y. Christian Intelligencer.*

Our extracts last week from this popular work, proved so acceptable that we have been induced to extend our approbation to some kindred topics.—*Home Journal.*

This exhaustive and admirable work defines Physiognomy and shows its benefits. It ought to find its way to every private and public library in the land.—*Herald of Health.*

Take such a volume as this, and every one must acknowledge that Physiognomy opens a wide field for interesting investigation.—*New York Daily Times.*

A work of great value. We particularly recommend it to artists.—*Philadelph. Press.*

We view it as a worthy addition to our library.—*American Educational Monthly.*

We cannot help treasuring the book as a highly valuable repository of practical wisdom, and of vast use to us in our course of life and action.—*N. Y. Jewish Messenger.*

The best work now extant upon the subject of Physiognomy, and that it is the most interesting one of the kind ever published, cannot be questioned.—*Chicago Even. Jour.*

It will take a place among the curiosities of literature and science.—*Palladium.*

This work is well worthy of a lengthened notice; but our space enables us to do little more than to commend it to the careful perusal of our readers.—*Scottish American.*

This the largest, and undoubtedly by far the best and most comprehensive work upon the subject of Physiognomy ever published.—*Chicago Prairie Farmer.*

No one can read the book with any degree of attention, without deriving much benefit from it, and its thorough study would furnish one with a knowledge of the signs of character indispensable to success in any walk of life.—*New Jerusalem Messenger.*

NEW PHYSIOGNOMY is a voluminous and very comprehensive work, taking the student by a thousand paths to a conclusion as to its entire correctness of theory, demonstrated by multitudes of the aptest illustrations.—*Boston Gazette.*

Those who already love to study character, will find this work a delightful companion; those who desire to acquire an insight into humanity by its outward signs, cannot find a better guide than in the illustrated NEW PHYSIOGNOMY.—*Phil. Sunday Times.*

It covers the whole ground more thoroughly than any book before issued.—*The Field.*

The author has thoroughly popularized his language, and is at home in his subject. The volume is full of materials from which thoughts are generated.—*Cin. Inquirer.*

In this volume, Mr. Wells, with a very full mastery of his subject, and in very pleasant style, takes in all the methods of conjecturing character from external signs. The work abounds with suggestive and often very instructive statements. Its tendency is decidedly in favor of moral right. In its department, NEW PHYSIOGNOMY is, of course, a standard, coming from the standard quarter.—*Methodist Quarterly Review.*

PRICE, MUSLIN, $5; HEAVY CALF, $8; TURKEY MOROCCO, GILT, ELEGANT, $10.

"IT IS AN ILLUSTRATED CYCLOPEDIA."

NEW PHYSIOGNOMY;

OR,

SIGNS OF CHARACTER,

As manifested in Temperament and External Forms, and especially in the Human Face Divine.

BY S. R. WELLS, EDITOR PHRENOLOGICAL JOURNAL.

Large 12mo, 768 pp. With more than 1,000 Engravings.

Illustrating Physiognomy, Anatomy, Physiology, Ethnology, Phrenology, and Natural History.

━━━━ ◆◆◆ ━━━━

A COMPREHENSIVE, thorough, and practical Work, in which all that is known on the subject treated is Systematized, Explained, Illustrated, and Applied. Physiognomy is here shown to be no mere fanciful speculation, but a consistent and well-considered system of Character-reading, based on the established truths of Physiology and Phrenology, and confirmed by Ethnology, as well as by the peculiarities of individuals. It is no abstraction, but something to be made useful; something to be practiced by everybody and in all places, and made an efficient help in that noblest of all studies—the Study of Man. It is readily understood and as readily applied. The following are some of the leading topics discussed and explained in this great illustrated work:

Previous Systems given, including those of all ancient and modern writers.

General Principles of Physiognomy, or the Physiological laws on which character-reading is and must be based.

Temperaments. — The Ancient Doctrines — Spurzheim's Description — The New Classification now in use here.

Practical Physiognomy. — General Forms of Faces—The Eyes, the Mouth, the Nose, the Chin, the Jaws and Teeth, the Cheeks, the Forehead, the Hair and Beard, the Complexion, the Neck and Ears, the Hands and Feet, the Voice, the Walk, the Laugh, the Mode of Shaking Hands, Dress, etc., with illustrations.

Ethnology.—The Races, including the Caucasian, the North American Indians, the Mongolian, the Malay, and the African, with their numerous subdivisions: also National Types, each illustrated.

Physiognomy Applied—To Marriage, to the Training of Children, to Personal Improvement, to Business, to Insanity and Idiocy, to Health and Disease, to Classes and Professions, to Personal Improvement, and to Character-Reading generally. Utility of Physiognomy, Self-Improvement.

Animal Types. — Grades of Intelligence, Instinct and Reason — Animal Heads and Animal Types among Men.

Graphomancy.—Character revealed in Hand-writing, with Specimens—Palmistry. "Line of Life" in the human hand.

Character-Reading. — More than a hundred noted Men and Women introduced—What Physiognomy says of them.

The Great Secret.—How to be Healthy and How to be Beautiful—Mental Cosmetics—very interesting, very useful.

Aristotle and St. Paul.—A Model Head—Views of Life — Illustrative Anecdotes—Detecting a Rogue by his Face.

━━━━━━━━

No one can read this Book without interest, without real profit. "Knowledge is power," and this is emphatically true of a knowledge of men—of human character. He who has it is "master of the situation;" and anybody may have it who will, and find in it the "secret of success" and the road to the largest personal improvement.

Price, in one large Volume, of nearly 800 pages, and more than 1,000 engravings, on toned paper, handsomely bound in embossed muslin, $5; in heavy calf, marbled edges, $8; Turkey morocco, full gilt, $10. Agents may do well to canvass for this work. Free by post. Please address, **S. R. WELLS, 389 Broadway, New York.**

"EDUCATION COMPLETE,"

Education and Self-Improvement Complete.—Comprising Physiology—Animal and Mental; Self-Culture and Perfection of Character; including the Management of Youth; Memory and Intellectual Improvement. Complete in one large, well-bound 12mo volume, with 855 pp., and upward of Seventy Engravings. Price, pre-paid, by mail, $4. Address SAMUEL R. WELLS, 389 Broadway, N. Y.

This work is, in all respects, one of the best educational hand-books in the English language. Any system of education that neglects the training and developing all that goes to make up a MAN, must necessarily be incomplete. The mind and body are so intimately related and connected, that it is impossible to cultivate the former without it is properly supplemented by the latter. The work is subdivided into three departments—the first, devoted to the preservation and restoration of health and the improvement of mentality; the second, to the regulation of the feelings and perfection of the moral character; and the third, to intellectual cultivation. "EDUCATION COMPLETE" is a library in itself, and covers the ENTIRE NATURE OF MAN. We append below a synopsis of the table of contents:

HEALTH OF BODY AND POWER OF MIND.

PHYSIOLOGY—ANIMAL AND MENTAL HEALTH—ITS LAWS AND PRESERVATION. Happiness constitutional; Pain not necessary; Object of all Education; Reciprocation existing between Body and Mind; Health Defined; Sickness—not providential.

FOOD—ITS NECESSITY AND SELECTION.—Unperverted Appetite an Infallible Directory; Different Diets Feed Different Powers; How to Eat—or Mastication, Quantity, Time, etc.; How Appetite can be Restrained; The Digestive Process; Exercise after Meals.

CIRCULATION, RESPIRATION, PERSPIRATION, SLEEP.—The Heart, its Structure and Office; The Circulatory System; The Lungs, their Structure and Functions, Respiration, and its importance; Perspiration; Prevention and Cure of Colds, and their consequences; Regulation of Temperature by Fire and Clothing; Sleep.

THE BRAIN AND NERVOUS SYSTEM.—Position, Function, and Structure of the Brain; Consciousness, or the seat of the soul; Function of the Nerves; How to keep the Nervous System in Health; The Remedy of Diseases; Observance of the Laws of Health Effectual; The Drink of Dyspeptics—its kind, time and quantity; Promotion of Circulation; Consumption—its Prevention and Cure; Preventives of Insanity, etc.

SELF-CULTURE AND PERFECTION OF CHARACTER.

CONSTITUENT ELEMENTS OR CONDITIONS OF PERFECTION OF CHARACTER.—Progression a Law of Things—its application to human improvement; Human perfectibility,—the harmonious action of all the faculties; Governing the propensities by the intellectual and moral faculties; Proof that the organs can be enlarged and diminished; The proper management of Youth, etc.

ANALYSIS AND MEANS OF STRENGTHENING OF THE FACULTIES.—Amativeness; Philoprogenitiveness; Adhesiveness; Union for Life; Inhabitiveness; Continuity; Vitativeness; Combativeness; Destructiveness, or Executiveness; Alimentiveness; Aquativeness, or Bibativeness; Acquisitiveness; Secretiveness; Cautiousness; Approbativeness; Self-Esteem; Firmness; Conscientiousness; Hope; Spirituality—Marvelousness; Veneration; Benevolence; Constructiveness; Ideality; Sublimity; Imitation; Mirthfulness; Agreeableness—with engraved illustrations.

MEMORY AND INTELLECTUAL IMPROVEMENT APPLIED TO SELF-EDUCATION.

CLASSIFICATION AND FUNCTIONS OF THE FACULTIES.—Man's superiority; Intellect his crowning endowment; How to strengthen and improve the Memory; Definition, location, analysis and means of strengthening he intellectual faculties. INDIVIDUALITY. FORM. SIZE. WEIGHT. COLOR. ORDER. CALCULATION. LOCALITY. EVENTUALITY. TIME. TUNE: Influence of music. LANGUAGE: Power of Eloquence; Good language. PHONOGRAPHY: its advantages. CAUSALITY: Teaching others to think; Astronomy; Anatomy and Physiology; Study of Nature. COMPARISON: Inductive reasoning. HUMAN NATURE: Adaptation.

DEVELOPMENTS REQUIRING FOR PARTICULAR AVOCATIONS.—Good Teachers; Clergymen; Physicians; Lawyers; Statesmen; Editors; Authors; Public Speakers; Poets; Lecturers; Merchants; Mechanics; Artists; Painters; Farmers; Engineers; Landlords; Printers; Milliners; Seamstresses; Fancy Workers, and the like.

Full and explicit directions are given for the cultivation and direction of all the powers of the mind, instruction for finding the exact location of each organ, and its relative size compared with others. A new edition of this great work has been recently printed, and may now be had in one volume. Agents in every neighborhood will be supplied in packages of a dozen or more copies by Express, or as Freight, at a discount. Single copies by mail. Address, SAMUEL R. WELLS, 389 Broadway, N. Y.

A LIST OF WORKS ON
Ethnology; or, Natural History of Man.

Types of Mankind; or, Ethnological Researches Based upon the Ancient Monuments, Paintings, Sculptures, and Crania of Races, and upon their Natural, Geographical, Philological, and Biblical History. Illustrated by Selections from the Unedited Papers of Samuel George Morton, M.D., and by additional contributions from Prof. L. Agassiz, LL.D., W. Usher, M.D., and Prof. H. S. Patterson, M.D. By J. C. Nott, M.D., and George R. Gliddon. $5; or by mail, $5 50.

Indigenous Races of the Earth; or, New Chapters of Ethnological Inquiry, including Monographs on Special Departments of Philology, Iconography, Cranioscopy, Palæontology, Pathology, Archæology, Comparative Geography, and Natural History. Contributed by Alfred Maury, Francis Pulsky, and J. A. Meigs, M.D. (with communications from Profs. Leidy and Agassiz), presenting Fresh Investigations, Documents, and Materials. By J. C. Nott, M.D., and George R. Gliddon. $5; by mail, $5 50.

Races of the Old World, a Manual of Ethnology. By C. L. Brace. $3 50.

The Origin of Species, by means of Natural Selection; or, the Preservation of Favored Races in the Struggle for Life. By Charles Darwin, M.A. $2 50.

The Origin of Species; or, the Causes of the Phenomena of Organic Nature. A Course of Six Lectures to Working-men. By Thomas H. Huxley. $1 25.

Huxley's Evidence as to Man's Place in Nature. $1 50.

Smith's Natural History of the Human Species; its Typical Forms, Primeval Distribution, Filiations, and Migrations. Illustrated. $2 00.

The Races of Man, and their Geographical Distribution. By Charles Pickering, M.D., to which is prefixed an Analytical Synopsis of the NATURAL HISTORY OF MAN. By J. C. Hall, M.D. $4 00.

Prichard's Natural History of Man, comprising Inquiries into the Modifying Influences of Physical and Moral Agencies on the Different Tribes of the Human Family. Fourth Edition, revised and enlarged. By Edwin Norris, of the Royal Asiatic Society. 2 vols. royal 8vo, with 62 colored plates, engraved on steel, and 100 engravings on wood. Cloth, $20 00.

Prichard's Six Ethnographical Maps. Supplement to the Natural History of Man, and to the Researches into the Physical History of Mankind. Folio, colored, and one sheet of letterpress. Second Edition. $10 00.

The Plurality of the Human Race. By Georges Pouchest. Translated and Edited by Hugh J. C. Beavan, F.R.G.S., F.A.S.L. $4 00.

Lake Habitations, and Pre-Historic Remains in the Turbaries and Marl-Beds of Northern and Central Italy. By Bartolomeo Gastaldi, Professor of Mineralogy in the College of Engineering at Turin. Translated from the Italian, and Edited by Charles Harcourt Chambers, M.A., F.R.G.S., F.A.S.L. $4 00.

The Anthropological Treatises of Johann Friedrich Blumenbach, with memories of him by Marx and Flourens, and an account of his Anthropological Museum by Professor R. Wagner, and the inaugural dissertation of John Hunter, M.D., on the Varieties of Man. Translated and Edited from the Latin, German, and French originals, by Thomas Bendyshe, M.A., V.P.A.S.L. $8.

Man's Origin and Destiny, Sketched from the Platform of the Sciences. A course of Lectures by J. P. Lesley. Illustrated. $1 00.

Man! Where, Whence, and Whither? Being a Glance at Man in his Natural History Relations. By David Page, F.R.S.E., F.G.S. $1 50.

The Illustrated Natural History of Man, in all Countries of the World. By Rev. J. G. Wood, M.A., F.L.S., with Illustrations by Wolf, Zwecker, and others. This work is being published in London in thirty-two monthly parts, twelve of which are now ready. Price, 50 cents each.

We keep in stock, or can supply to order, all of the above and any other works on this interesting and important subject. Address,

S. R. WELLS, Publisher, 389 Broadway, New York.

ORATORY—SACRED AND

Or, the EXTEMPORANEOUS SPEAKER. Including a
for conducting Public Meetings according to the best Parl
WM. PITTENGER, with an Introduction by Hon. JOHN A. B1
and succinct Exposition of the Rules and Methods of Practic
in the Expression of Thought, and an acceptable style, may
composition and gesture. Beveled boards. One handsom
pages, tinted paper, post-paid, $1 50. S. R. WELLS, publish

This book aspires to a place which has hitherto been vacant
Many works describe the external qualities of an oration, and
stance. Not more than one or two embrace both departments
by which thoughts, that may be very vague at first, find expr
powerfully spoken words. And even these are deficient in illu
practical directions for the student, as well as diffuse and obscur
the whole field, and shows in a plain and simple style how ever
of successful speech may be removed. The following sketch w
the purpose of the book.

The different kinds of oratory—some six in all—from the full
unpremeditated, are considered, and the preference given to th
is carefully pre-arranged and the words extemporized. This p
enforced by Hon. JOHN A. BINGHAM, who shows, in an able i
extemporaneous speaking is the most natural and therefore the

Several chapters are devoted to *general preparation*, a subjec
for while men undergo long courses of training for trades and
often thought to be accessible without previous culture. The 1
sary for efficient speech are specified at length, and full directior
their efficiency and acquiring the knowledge necessary to for1
quence. In this section a mass of valuable information and sug;
which could not easily be found elsewhere, and the whole enliv
dotes of speakers remarkable for their possession of the quali
their lack of them.

Parts Second and Third treat of the preparation and deliv
courses. The divers embarrassments and exigencies that may
speech are discussed with a clearness of insight which implies
have met them in his own experience. Chapter fourth, which
stages of a discourse, can not be read by the practiced speaker
ings like those of an old soldier when he listens to a well-told
Hints are given for all departments of address from preaching
scarcely any one whose manner of speech is not unalterably 1
something that may be of advantage to him.

Part Fourth is, perhaps, generally, the most interesting of the
of the more characteristic achievements of celebrated speaker:
ticular accounts of their modes of preparation. Many of th
directly from the speakers themselves, and their testimony j
favor of unwritten eloquence.

The Chairman's Guide, or rules of order, adapted to the cond
public meetings, is condensed into an appendix. Nothing of 1
mentary usage is omitted, and the whole thrown into a very co
form. This feature will be found of great value to those par
societies, debating clubs, or other assemblies.

The book is written in a compact but graceful style, and fror
thoroughly readable. We confidently believe that the public wil
province, to be the best and most useful American treatise yet pr
nal appearance of the volume is very fine. Its handsome bindi
clear type are in perfect correspondence with the permanent val

Address S. R. WELLS, Publisher, 389 Broad

Life in the West.*

Besides a general description of the Western States—from Minnesota to Texas, and from the Ohio River to the Rocky Mountains—the author, N. C. M., of ——, correspondent of the New York *Tribune*, and now Agricultural Editor of that journal, has given us, in a handy volume, such a fund of knowledge as can be found nowhere else. Read the author's brief PREFACE:

" A long residence in the Mississippi Valley, frequent journeys through its whole extent, and years of service as the Illinois correspondent of the New York *Tribune*, have furnished the materials for the following stories. Within forty years a country has been developed equal to the whole of Western Europe; new habits and customs prevail; families about to be extinguished have received new vigor, and the lowly have been exalted. Innumerable cities, towns, and villages have arisen, and more than a million of highly productive farms have been brought into cultivation. Results must follow which will be different from any the world has yet seen, because wealth, having ceased to descend to the oldest son, is divided among many. In no other country have the producers been able to keep so much wealth from the grasp of the idle and wicked, and devote it to the education of their children and to making home comfortable.

" One language is spoken, knowledge and industrious habits are universal, and the religious sentiment guides. A soil of remarkable fertility, a climate rich in sunshine and showers, give abundance of food; and orchards and vineyards abound. Thousands of families, by their own industry, have created beautiful homes, and they sit at tables spread with as good—with as varied food—as any king can command with his slaves and gold. Did the shadow of a king stretch across that region, the red man and his game would linger still. No sentiment is stronger than a love for the Union founded on freedom. Were it possible for the nations of Europe or Asia to unite, they could not become as wealthy, as intelligent, and as powerful as ours is destined to become, with its center in the Mississippi Valley.

" From our new conditions we have new ideas, and they will impress themselves on the society of the whole of the two American continents. What this impress shall be, may, in some degree, be gathered from an account of the labors and hopes, from the disappointments and triumphs, and from the sorrows and joys in families.

" In the Eastern States, educated persons look on the comic and burlesque exhibited in the Western character as an evidence of a want of culture. Difficulties and labors which appall the refined, in the West have been overcome. During the hours of darkness and doubt, relaxation was a necessity; free from restraint and unfettered by rules, a cultivated cheerfulness ran into the comic. These things had their origin in the Atlantic States, and they are new as one's children are new."

Even we, who have seen something of the West, can not fully comprehend its extent, its richness, its vastness, and its future influence on civilization. We can only predict something great, something much beyond present comprehension. The book under notice deals chiefly with its past and its present, leaving its future with other historians, who will have something more to record. Though not a novel, in its general sense, this work will prove no less fascinating than the best romance.

* LIFE IN THE WEST; or, Stories of the Mississippi Valley. By N. C. Meeker, Agricultural Editor of the New York *Tribune*. One large 12mo volume; pp. 356. Price $2. Published by SAMUEL R. WELLS, 389 Broadway, New York.

Gymnastics and Physical Culture.

We give below a complete list of the best works on this all-important subject. We are also agents for Bacon's "Home Gymnasium;" supply Indian Clubs and all Gymnastic apparatus. Price list contained in our new Illustrated and Descriptive Catalogue, sent to any address on receipt of two red stamps. S. R. WELLS, 389 Broadway, New York.

Illustrated Family Gymnasium.—Containing the most improved methods of applying Gymnastic, Calisthenic, Kinesipathic, and Vocal Exercises to the Development of the Bodily Organs, the Invigoration of their Functions, the Preservation of Health, and the Cure of Disease and Deformities. With numerous illustrations. By R. T. Trall, M.D., author of "Hydropathic Encyclopedia," etc. $1 75.

New Gymnastics, for Men, Women, and Children. By Dio Lewis, M.D. A new, revised, and enlarged edition. $1 75.

Weak Lungs, and How to make them Strong; or, Diseases of the Organs of the Chest, with their Home Treatment by the Movement-Cure. By Dio Lewis, M.D. Illustrated. $1 75.

Physical Perfection; or, the Philosophy of Human Beauty—showing How to Acquire and Retain Bodily Symmetry, Health, and Vigor, Secure Long Life, and Avoid the Infirmities and Deformities of Age. By D H. Jacques. $1 75.

Manual of Physical Exercises, comprising Gymnastics, Calisthenics, Rowing, Sailing, Skating, Swimming, Fencing, Sparring, Cricket, Base Ball, etc.; together with Rules for Training, and Sanitary Suggestions. By William Wood. $1 50.

Manual of Calisthenics, a Systematic Drill-Book without Apparatus, for Schools, Families, and Gymnasiums, with Music to accompany the Exercises. Illustrated from Original Designs. By J. M. Watson. $1 25.

Hand-Book of Calisthenics and Gymnastics, a Complete Drill-Book for Schools, Families, and Gymnasiums, with Music to accompany the Exercises. Illustrated from Original Designs. By J. M. Watson $2 25.

The Indian Club Exercise, with Explanatory Figures and Positions, Photographed from Life; also, General Remarks on Physical Culture. Illustrated with Portraitures of celebrated Athletes, exhibiting great Muscular Development from the Club Exercise, engraved from photographs expressly for this work. $2 50.

Manual of Light Gymnastics, for Instruction in Classes and Private Use. With numerous illustrations. By W. L. Rathe. 40 cents.

A Hand-Book of Gymnastics and Athletics. By E. G. Ravenstein and John Hulley. $5 00.

Calisthenics; or, the Elements of Bodily Culture on Pestalozzian Principles, Designed for Practical Education in Schools, Colleges, Families, etc. By Henry de Laspée. Illustrated with Two Thousand Figures. $12 00.

Physiology and Calisthenics, for Schools and Families. By Catharine E. Beecher. Illustrated with many Physiological and other cuts. $1 00.

An Illustrated Sketch of the Movement-Cure, its Principles, Methods, and Effects. By George H. Taylor, M.D. 25 cents.

An Exposition of the Swedish Movement-Cure. Embracing the History and Philosophy of this System of Medical Treatment, with Examples of Single Movements, and Directions for their Use in Various Forms of Chronic Diseases; forming a Complete Manual of Exercises, together with a Summary of the Principles of General Hygiene. By George H. Taylor, A.M., M.D. $1 75.

Theory and Practice of the Movement-Cure; or, the Treatment of Lateral Curvature of the Spine; Paralysis, Indigestion, Constipation; Consumption; Angular Curvatures, and other Deformities, Diseases Incident to Women; Derangements of the Nervous System, and other Chronic Affections, by the Swedish System of Localized Movements. By Charles F. Taylor, M.D. Illustrated. $1 75.

Prevention and Cure of Consumption, by the Swedish Movement-Cure; with Directions for its Home Application. By D. Wark, M.D. 30 cents.

The Swedish Movement-Cure. What It Is and What It Can Do. By William W. Wier, M.D. 25 cents.

Sent by mail, post-paid, on receipt of price. Address,

S. R. WELLS, Publisher, 389 Broadway, New York.

LIBRARY

OF

MESMERISM AND PSYCHOLOGY.

COMPLETE IN ONE LARGE VOLUME.

" All are but parts of one stupendous whole,
Whose body nature is, and God the soul."

Comprising the PHILOSOPHY OF MESMERISM, CLAIRVOYANCE, MENTAL ELEC-TRICITY.—FASCINATION, or the Power of Charming· Illustrating the Principles of Life in connection with Spirit and Matter.—THE MACROCOSM AND MICRO-COSM, or the Universe Without and Universe Within : being an unfolding of the plan of Creation, and the Correspondence of Truths, both in the World of Sense and the World of Soul.—THE PHILOSOPHY OF ELECTRICAL PSYCHOLOGY ; the Doctrine of Impressions ; including the connection between Mind and Matter ; also, the Treatment of Disease.—PSYCHOLOGY, or the Science of the Soul, consid-ered Physiologically and Philosophically ; with an appendix containing notes of Mesmeric and Psychical experience, and illustrations of the Brain and Nervous System.

In this LIBRARY is embraced all the most practical matter yet written on these deeply interesting, though somewhat mysterious, subjects. Having these works at hand, the reader may learn all there is known of MESMERISM, CLAIRVOYANCE, BIOLOGY, and PSYCHOLOGY. He may also learn how to produce results which the most scientific men have not yet been able to explain. The *facts* are here recorded, and the practice or *modus operandi* given. In order to give an idea of the scope of the work, we append a brief synopsis of the table of contents :

Charming—How to Charm ; Fascination ; Double Life of Man ; Spiritual States ; Stages in Dying ; Operation of Medicine ; What is Prevision, or Second Sight ? Philosophy of Somnambulism ; History of Fascination ; Beecher on Magnetism ; Electrical Psychology—its Definition and Importance in Curing Disease ; Mind and Matter ; The Existence of a Deity Proved ; Subject of Creation Considered ; The Doctrine of Impressions ; The Secret Revealed, so that all may know how to Experiment without an Instructor ; Electro-Biology ; Genetology, or Human Beauty Philosophically Considered ; Philosophy of Mesmerism ; Animal Magnetism ; Mental Electricity, or Spiritualism ; The Philosophy of Clairvoyance ; Degrees in Mesmerism ; Psychology ; Origin, Phenomena, Physiology, Philosophy and Psychol-ogy of Mesmerism ; Mesmeric and Physical Experience ; Clairvoyance as applied to Physiology and Medicine ; Trance, or Spontaneous Ecstasies ; The Practice and Use of Mesmerism and Circles ; The Doctrine of Degrees ; Doctrine of Cor-respondences ; Doctrine of Progressive Development ; Law Agency and Divine Agency ; Providences, etc., etc., with other interesting matter.

The LIBRARY contains several works by different authors, making some Nine Hundred pages, nicely printed and substantially and handsomely bound in one portly 12mo volume. Price for the work, complete, pre-paid by return of post, $4.

Address, SAMUEL R. WELLS, 389 Broadway, New York.

Food and Diet.

A Practical Treatise. With Observations on the Dietetical Regimen, suited for Disordered States of the Digestive Organs, and an account of the Dietaries of some of the Principal Metropolitan and other Establishments for Paupers, Lunatics, Criminals, Children, the Sick, etc. By JONATHAN PEREIRA, M.D., F.R.S., and L.S. Edited by CHARLES A. LEE, M.D. Octavo, 318 pp., with full Table of Contents and new Index complete. Muslin, $1 75. Sent free by first post. Address, S. R. WELLS, Publisher, 389 Broadway, New York.

An important physiological work. Considerable pains have been taken in the preparation of tables representing the proportion of some of the chemical elements, and of the alimentary principles contained in different foods, the time required for digestion, etc. Among the subjects treated and analyzed are the following, in alphabetical order:

Abstemious diet; acidity of stomach, causes; agricultural laborers, average quantity of food; air; albumen, composition; alcohol, action on the liver; alcoholic alimentary principle; ale, Indian pale; alimentary principles whose oxygen and hydrogen are in the same ratio as in water; alimentiveness, or the propensity to eat and drink; alkali, concrete acidulated; allspice; almonds, sweet and bitter; ammonia, in the atmosphere; amontillado; antiscorbutic acids, lemon juice; apples; apricot; army rations; arrow-root—East Indian, English, Portland, Tahiti; arsenic in bones; artesian wells; artichoke, the garden, the Jerusalem; asafœtida; asparagus; azote, see nitrogen.

Baccate or berried fruits; barley bread, Scotch, water, compound; batatas; bean—broad, garden, kidney, scarlet, Windsor; beef flesh; beer; beer-topers and spirit-tipplers, difference between; bees; beetroot; bile, assists the chymification of oils and fats; birds—eggs, fat of, the aquatic, the dark-fleshed, the rapacious, the white-fleshed, viscera of; biscuit, meal; biscuits—Abernethy, buttered; blood, corpuscles; boiling, loss of weight in; bones; brandy; bread—adulteration of, barley, black, brown, compressed, gluten, loaf, new, oat, piled or flaky, pudding, formula for unfermented, patent unfermented, ship, unfermented or unleavened, wheat; breads —of the light and elastic—(spongy) unfermented; breakfast; Bright's farina; broccoli; broiling; broths and soups; Burgundy wine; butchers' meat; butter, cause of its becoming rancid; milk.

Cabbage, lettuces; cacao; caffeine; cakes, plum; calcium; calf's sweetbread; caramel; carbon; carbonic acid, production of, in the system; carrageen, or Irish moss; carrot; caseine, animal; caseum; cauliflower; celery; cellular tissue of mammals; cereal grains; cerebric acid; Ceylon or Jafna moss; champagne; cheese; cherry; chestnut; chicken; chiccory; chloride of sodium, potassium; chlorine; chocolate; choleic acid; cinnamon; citron; claret wines; clay, eaten as a luxury; climate; cloves; cocoa; cod liver oil; cockles; coffee; condiments or seasoning agents; constipation, diet for; cooking, loss in; corn; crawfish; cows' heels; crab; cranberry; cream; crustaceans; cucumber; Curaçoa; curd; currants, red and black,

Dates; dextrine; diabetes, diet for; diastase; diet—animal, fish, for diabetic patients; dietaries—for children, emigrants, paupers, prisoners, puerperal women, insane, sick, foundlings, orphans, London Lying-in Hospital, Infant Orphan Asylum, soldiers', naval service; digestion; dinner; drinks—acidulous, alcoholic and other intoxicating, aromatic or astringent, containing gelatine or liquid aliments; duck; eating—times of, repose after, conduct before, at, after; eels; eggs —can not support life, white or glaire, yolk; elderberry; ergotism.

Farina; fats, animal; farinaceous food for infants, or starchy substances; fermentation, digestive; ferns; ferrotypes; fibrine, animal; fig; fish—diet, methods of preserving, poison, poisonous species of, the roe or ovary of, the viscera of; fishes; flounder; flour, wheaten; fluorine; flummery; food consumed by and excretions of a horse in 24 hours; animal food—digestibility, circumstances, chemical elements, quantity of, at a meal, refusal of, by lunatics, solid and liquid, nutritive qualities of, vegetable; fowl; fruits—aurantiaceous, cucurbitaceous, drupaceous, or stone, fleshy, leguminous; frying; fungi or mushrooms; fur of tea-kettles.

Garlic; gastric juice; gelatine altered by heat; gelatinous alimentary principle, substances; gin; ginger beer; gingerbread; globules of the blood; glue; gluten; glutinous matter; goose—fattening of, fatty liver of, gooseberries; gormandizing powers of the natives of the Arctic Regions; gourds; grape, the—juice, sugar; greens; gruel; gums; gum-arabic lozenges; gypsum, eaten, in water.

Haddock, the; hartshorn; hazel-nut; hemp, Indian; herring; horse, food consumed by; hydrogen.

Iceland moss; Indian corn starch; indigestion, diet for; iron; isinglass, varieties of.

Jams; jellies, fruit; jelly, calf's foot; Jerusalem artichoke.

Ketchup; kidney.

Lactic acid; leeks; leguminous fruits; lemonade; lemon and kali; lentils; lichenin, or feculoid; lime; limpets; liquid aliments, or drinks; liquorice; liver, fatty, of the goose, the frequency of diseases of in tropical climates; lobster, the.

Macaroni; Madeira; magnesium; maize, or Indian corn; malt, liquor; meat—butchers', salted, white; milk—animal, artificial asses', cocoa-nut, cows', cream of, ewes', goats', quantity of cream in cows'; molasses and treacle; mollusks; morel, common; moss—carrageen, or Irish, Ceylon, or Jaffna; mucilage; mulberry; muscle; muscular flesh; mushroom, field or cultivated; mussels, oysters, deleterious effects; mustard; mutton.

Nectarine; nitrogenized foods; nutmeg.

Oats; oat-bread, unfermented; oatmeal porridge; obesity, mode of promoting; oil—Florence, olive, or sweet; oils, essential or volatile; onion; opium; orange; organic tissues; ox, liver of the; oxalic acid; oxygen, consumption in respiration; oyster.

Packwax; panada; pancakes; parsley; pastry; peas; peach; pemmican; pepper; pepsine; periwinkles; pineapple; plum; pomaceous fruits, or apples; port wine; porter; potash; salts; potassium; potato flour; powders—ginger-beer, soda, seidlitz; prawns and shrimps; preserves; prunes; pudding; putrescent matter, ill effects of.

Quina; quince.

Rabbit; raisins; raspberry; rataflas; rations, army; receptacles and bracts; rennet; reptiles; rhubarb; rice; roasted flesh; rolls, hot; rum; rusks; rye—bread, ergot, pottage.

Saccharine alimentary principle; sago; saline alimentary principle; salmon; salt, common; scallops; scurvy; seeds, mealy or farinaceous; semolina, sherry; smelts; snails; snow; soda powders; souchy, water; sourkrout, or sauerkraut; spinage; sponge; sprats; starch; stirabout; strawberry; stuff, used by bakers; suet puddings; sugar—an element of respiration, boiled, brown, burnt, candy, crystal; sulphur; sulphureted hydrogen of water; sweetwort.

Tasters, wine; tamarind; tapioca; tea; theine; tickor; tops and bottoms; tripe; truffle, common; turbot; turnips; turtle.

Universal sanative breakfast beverage.

Veal; vegetable, adapted for divers; fibrine; venison; vermicelli; vinegar.

Water—as a dietetical remedy, barley, purification of, common, tests of the usual impurities in, impregnated with lead, lake, marsh, of the Dead Sea, preservation of at sea, rain, river, sea, snow, spring; waters—carbonated or acidulous, mineral, chalybeate or ferraginous, sulphureous or hepatic, the alkaline, the brine, the calcareous, the silicious; water-melon; wheat; wheaten bread; wheaten flour; whelks; whey—alum, cream of tartar; white bait; whisky; wines, their uses.

Zeiger; zymome, and so forth.

Together with much other matter which every one should know who eats to live, instead of living to eat. The book is thoroughly scientific, and the best authority on the subject. Sent by return post on receipt of price, by S. R. WELLS, 389 Broadway, New York. AGENTS WANTED.

THE INDISPENSABLE HAND-BOOK.

How to Write----How to Talk----How to Behave, and How to Do Business.

COMPLETE IN ONE LARGE VOLUME.

THIS new work—in four parts—embraces just that practical matter-of-fact information which every one—old and young—ought to have. It will aid in attaining, if it does not insure, "success in life." It contains some 600 pages, elegantly bound, and is divided into four parts, as follows:

How to Write:

AS A MANUAL OF LETTER-WRITING AND COMPOSITION, IS FAR SUPERIOR to the common "Letter-Writers." It teaches the inexperienced how to write Business Letters, Family Letters, Friendly Letters, Love Letters, Notes and Cards, and News-paper Articles, and how to Correct Proof for the Press. The newspapers have pronounced it "Indispensable."

How to Talk:

NO OTHER BOOK CONTAINS SO MUCH USEFUL INSTRUCTION ON THE subject as this. It teaches how to Speak Correctly, Clearly, Fluently, Forcibly, Eloquently, and Effectively, in the Shop, in the Drawing-room; a Chairman's Guide, to conduct Debating Societies and Public Meetings; how to Spell, and how to Pronounce all sorts of Words; with Exercises for Declamation. The chapter on "Errors Corrected" is worth the price of the volume to every young man. "Worth a dozen grammars."

How to Behave:

THIS IS A MANUAL OF ETIQUETTE, AND IT IS BELIEVED TO BE THE best "MANNERS BOOK" ever written. If you desire to know what good manners require, at Home, on the Street, at a Party, at Church, at Table, in Conversation, at Places of Amusement, in Traveling, in the Company of Ladies, in Courtship, this book will inform you. It is a standard work on Good Behavior.

How to Do Business:

INDISPENSABLE IN THE COUNTING-ROOM, IN THE STORE, IN THE SHOP, on the FARM, for the Clerk, the Apprentice, the Book Agent, and for Business Men. It teaches how to Choose a Pursuit, and how to follow it with success. "It teaches how to get rich honestly," and how to use your riches wisely.

How to Write—How to Talk—How to Behave—How to Do Business, bound in one large handsome volume, post-paid, for $2 25.

Agents wanted. Address, **S. R. WELLS, 389 Broadway, New York.**

THE
NEW TESTAMENT

IN GREEK AND ENGLISH,

ENTITLED

THE EMPHATIC DIAGLOTT,

Containing the Original Greek Text of what is commonly called THE NEW TESTAMENT, with an Interlineary Word-for-word English Translation ; a New Emphatic Version based on the Interlineary Translation, on the Readings of Eminent Critics, and on the various Readings of the Vatican Manuscript (No. 1,209 in the Vatican Library) ; together with Illustrative and Explanatory Foot Notes, and a copious Selection of References ; to the whole of which is added a valuable Alphabetical Index   By Benjamin Wilson. One vol., 12mo, pp. 884.   Price, $4 ; extra fine binding, $5.   SAMUEL R. WELLS, Publishers, 389 Broadway, New York.

This valuable work is now complete.   The different renderings of various passages in the New Testament are the foundations on which most of the sects of Christians have been built up.   Without claiming absolute correctness for our author's new and elaborate version, we present his work so that each reader may judge for himself whether the words there literally translated are so arranged in the common version as to express the exact meaning of the New Testament writers.

In regard to Mr. Wilson's translation there will doubtless be differences of opinion among Greek scholars, but having submitted it to several for examination, their verdict has been so generally in its favor that we have no hesitation in presenting it to the public.

We have no desire for sectarian controversy, and believe that it is consequent chiefly upon misinterpretation, or upon variations in the formal presentation of the truths of *Christianity* as taught in the New Testament ; and it is with the earnest desire that what appears crooked shall be made straight, that we present this volume to the careful consideration of an intelligent people.

OPINIONS OF THE CLERGY.

The following extracts from letters just received by the publishers from some of our most eminent divines will go far to show in what light the new "Emphatic Diaglott" is regarded by the clergy in general :

From THOMAS ARMITAGE, D.D., *Pastor of the Fifth Avenue Baptist Church.*—"GENTLEMEN: I have examined with much care and great interest the specimen sheets sent me of 'The Emphatic Diaglott.' * * * I believe that the book furnishes evidences of purposed faithfulness, more than usual scholarship, and remarkable literary industry.   It can not fail to be an important help to those who wish to become better acquainted with the revealed will of God.   For these reasons I wish the enterprise of publishing the work great success."

From REV. JAMES L. HODGE, *Pastor of the First Mariner's Baptist Church, N. Y.*—"I have examined these sheets which you design to be a specimen of the work, and have to confess myself much pleased with the arrangement and ability of Mr. Wilson. * * * I can most cordially thank Mr. Wilson for his noble work, and you, gentlemen, for your Christian enterprise in bringing the work before the public.   I believe the work will do good, and aid in the better understanding of the New Testament."

From SAMUEL OSGOOD, D.D., *New York City.*—"I have looked over the specimen of the new and curious edition of the New Testament which you propose publishing, and think that it will be a valuable addition to our Christian literature.   It is a work of great labor and careful study, and without being sure of agreeing with the author in all his views, I can commend his book to all lovers of Biblical research."

ÆSOP'S FABLES.

Style of Engraving—THE FROG AND THE OX.

Æsop's Fables Illustrated.—The People's Pictorial Edition. With Seventy Splendid Illustrations. Complete in one vol., 12mo, 72 pp. Beautifully printed on tinted paper, bound in cloth, gilt edges, beveled boards, $1.

The following brief selections, from a very numerous collection of notices of the Press, show with what favor this beautiful edition has been received.

The New York *Daily Times* says: " This attractive volume is very appropriately styled ' The People's Edition.' The illustrations are numerous, spirited, and well engraved."

The *Christian Intelligencer* says: " The designs are new, apt, and form a decided feature of this work. The artist has put wit into his delineations, and the fables may be read *in their pictorial representatives.*"

The Cincinnati *Journal of Commerce* says: " It is an exceedingly beautiful little volume, and is well worthy of having a place in every house with the family Bible."

The Brooklyn *Union* says: " It is one of the best gift-books of the season."

The *American Baptist* says: " It is a neat volume, beautifully illustrated. It contains a larger number of fables than we have before seen grouped together under the name of that great master."

The *Rural New Yorker* says: " The form, appearance and general style of the book make it truly ' The People's Edition,' as the publishers announce."

The *Mount Holly Herald* says: " It is gotten up in sumptuous style, and illustrated with great beauty of design. It will conduce to educate the eye and elevate the taste of the young to the appreciation of the highest and most perfect forms of grace and beauty."

The *Phrenological Journal* says: " This is a beautiful edition of the sayings of the slave of Athens. The volume is complete, containing over TWO HUNDRED FABLES and upward of SIXTY FINE-LINED WOOD ENGRAVINGS, NEARLY EVERY PAGE BEING CHARMINGLY ILLUSTRATED. IT IS BEAUTIFULLY PRINTED ON TINTED PAPER, BOUND IN CLOTH, WITH GILT EDGES, AND WELL CALCULATED FOR A POPULAR GIFT TO OLD AND YOUNG."

ANATOMICAL AND PHYSIOLOGICAL PLATES.

New Anatomical and Physiological Plates for Lecturers, Physicians, and Others. By R. T. TRALL, M. D., author of various works.

These plates represent all the organs and principal structures of the human body *in situ*, and of the size of life. There are six in the set, backed and on rollers, as follows:

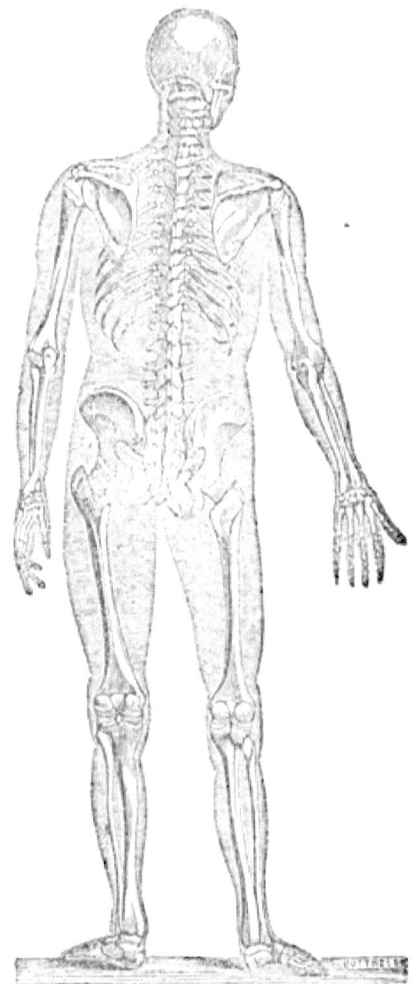

The Heart and Lungs.—No. 1 presents a front view of the lungs, heart, stomach, liver, gall-bladder, larynx, thymus, and parotid glands, common carotid arteries, and jugular vein. Colored as in life.

Dissections.—No. 2 is a complete dissection of the heart, exhibiting its valves and cavities, and the course of the blood. The large arteries and the veins of the heart, lungs, and neck are displayed, with the windpipe and its bronchial ramifications; also the liver with its gall-bladder and ducts; the pancreas; the kidneys with their ureters and blood vessels; the descending aorta, or large artery of the chest and abdomen; ovaries, fallopian tubes, round and broad ligaments, etc.

Nervous System.—No. 3. Side view of the brain, heart, lungs, liver, bowels, uterus, and bladder. Also the various subdivisions of the base of the brain, with the whole length of the spinal cord, showing the origin of all the cerebro-spinal nerves.

The Eye and the Ear.—No. 4. The anatomy of the eye and ear, representing the arrangements of the minute blood-vessels, nerves, and other structures concerned in the functions of seeing and hearing.

Digestion.—No. 5. The alimentary canal, exhibiting the exact size, shape, and arrangements of structures especially concerned in digestion, viz.: the mouth, throat, tongue, esophagus, stomach, small and large intestines, with the liver, gall-bladder, and the biliary ducts; also the internal structure of the kidneys, and a beautiful representation of the lacteal absorbents and glands, thoracic duct, and their connections with the thoracic arteries and veins.

Circulation—Skin.—No. 6. The lobes of the lungs and cavities of the heart, valves, etc., with the large vessels of the circulation; also a minute dissection of the structures of the skin—the sebaceous follicles, sweat glands, etc.; exhibiting the extent and importance of the great depurating functions of the surface.

Every lecturer, teacher, and physician should have a set. Price for the whole, beautifully colored and mounted, $20. We do not sell single plates. May be sent by Express. Address SAMUEL R. WELLS, No. 389 Broadway, New York.

[That the reader may judge of the value of this capital HAND BOOK, we append the Table of Contents for the different years, *from number one*, as follows:]

C O N T E N T S

OF

The Illustrated Annuals of Phrenology & Physiognomy,

FOR

1 8 6 5

1 8 6 6 .

1 8 6 7 .

1 8 6 8 .

BACON'S PATENT HOME GYMNASIUM.

The only complete portable Gymnasium ever invented. Invaluable to those of sedentary occupations. No home should be without one. Put up in any room, and removed in a minute.

All complete Gymnasiums that have been previously constructed, have been too cumbrous or too expensive; and those of a cheap and simple character have been lacking in the necessary scope and variety, not being adapted to swinging or somersault exercises. Many attempts have been made to construct one which would overcome these difficulties, and this we now claim to have accomplished in our PATENT HOME GYMNASIUM. It is based on the principles devised and taught by Ling, Schreber, and Dio Lewis, and is a combination of these systems brought into a small compass. While the first exercises are simple enough for children, the last are such as only can be accomplished by the most athletic. It is believed that this apparatus—being cheap, portable, and adapted to all—will be the means through which Gymnastics will become universal.

This apparatus is supported by two strong hooks in the ceiling, eighteen inches apart, and screwed into the joist five inches, leaving only the small hooks visible. It can also be used in a yard, by the erection of a framework such as is used for swings. The straps are of the strongest linen, handsomely colored, and by an ingenious device, the rings and stirrups can be instantly raised or lowered to any desired height. A space six or eight feet wide is ample for any of the exercises. The apparatus can also be converted into a Trapeze for the athlete, or a swing for the juvenile.

Price of the complete Gymnasium, with four large sheets of illustrations (100 cuts), and Hand-book explaining how each is performed $10 00
The Trapeze adjustment, with thirty-two illustrations 3 50
The Swing adjustment 1 50

Sent by Express to any part of the United States or Canada, on receipt of price.

Kehoe's Improved Indian Clubs.—Used by the Principal Gymnasts in the United States. Weights, from six to fifty pounds each. The best in use.

6, 7 and 8 lbs. each, per pair . . $5 50	15 lbs. each, per pair . . . $10 00
10 lbs. " " " . . 6 50	20 " " " . . . 14 00
12 " " " . . 7 00	25 " " " . . . 16 00

SIZES FOR LADIES AND CHILDREN.

2 lbs. each, per pair . . . $2 00	4 lbs. each, per pair . . . $3 50
3 " " " . . . 3 00	5 " " " . . . 5 00

Dumb Bells, Rings, Wands, etc., for Light Gymnastics; Croquet—parlor and lawn.

BOOKS ON PHYSICAL DEVELOPMENT.

Trall's Family Gymnasium. Illustrated . . .	$1 75
Dio Lewis's Light Gymnastics. Adapted to all . .	1 75
Physical Perfection; Or, How to be Beautiful . .	1 75
Watson's Hand-Book of Calisthenics. Illustrated .	2 25
Watson's Manual of Calisthenics. Illustrated . .	1 25
Kehoe's Indian Club Exercise. (Illustrated Hand-Book) .	2 50
Taylor's Movement-Cure; Or, The Treatment of Disease .	1 75
Dio Lewis's Weak Lungs, and How to Make them Strong .	1 75
Wood's Physical Exercises. Illustrated	1 50
The Lifting Cure. Butler's System, ...	1 00

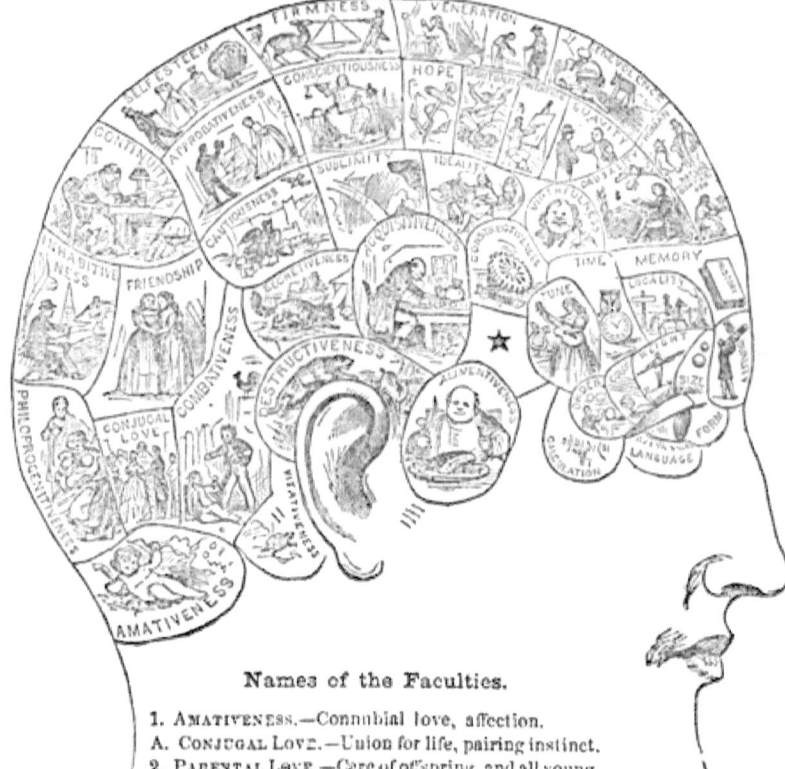

Names of the Faculties.

1. AMATIVENESS.—Connubial love, affection.
A. CONJUGAL LOVE.—Union for life, pairing instinct.
2. PARENTAL LOVE.—Care of offspring, and all young.
3. FRIENDSHIP.—Sociability, union of friends.
4. INHABITIVENESS.—Love of home and country.
5. CONTINUITY.—Application, consecutiveness.

E. VITATIVENESS.—Clinging to life, tenacity.
6. COMBATIVENESS.—Defense, courage.
7. DESTRUCTIVENESS.—Executiveness.
8. ALIMENTIVENESS.—Appetite for food, etc.
9. ACQUISITIVENESS.—Frugality, economy.
10. SECRETIVENESS.—Self-control, policy.
11. CAUTIOUSNESS.—Guardedness, safety.
12. APPROBATIVENESS.—Love of applause.
13. SELF-ESTEEM.—Self-respect, dignity.
14. FIRMNESS.—Stability, perseverance.
15. CONSCIENTIOUSNESS.—Sense of right.
16. HOPE.—Expectation, anticipation.
17. SPIRITUALITY.—Intuition, prescience.
18. Veneration—Worship, adoration.
19. BENEVOLENCE.—Sympathy, kindness.
20. CONSTRUCTIVENESS.—Ingenuity, tools.
21. IDEALITY.—*Taste*, love of beauty, poetry.
B. SUBLIMITY.—Love of the grand, vast.
22. IMITATION.—Copying, aptitude.
23. MIRTH.—Fun, wit, ridicule, facetiousness.
24. INDIVIDUALITY.—Observation, to see.

25. FORM.—Memory, *shape*, looks, persons.
26. SIZE.—Measurement of quantity.
27. WEIGHT.—Control of motion, balancing.
28. COLOR.—Discernment, and love of color.
29. ORDER.—*Method*, system, going by *rule*.
30. CALCULATION.—Mental arithmetic.
31. LOCALITY.—Memory of place, position.
32. EVENTUALITY.—Memory of facts, events.
33. TIME.—Telling *when*, time of day, dates.
34. TUNE.—Love of music, singing.
35. LANGUAGE.—*Expression* by words, acts.
36. CAUSALITY.—*Planning*, thinking.
37. COMPARISON.—Analysis, inferring.
C. HUMAN NATURE.—Sagacity.
D. SUAVITY.—*Pleasantness*, blandness.

———————

For complete definitions of all the organs of the BRAIN, and all the features of the FACE, see **New Physiognomy** by S. R. WELLS, with 1,000 illustrations. Price, post-paid, $5, $8, and $10, according to styles of binding.

Phrenology and its Uses.

PHRENOLOGY is the most *useful* of all modern discoveries; for while others enhance creature comforts mainly, this Science teaches LIFE and its LAWS, and unfolds human nature in all its aspects. Its fundamental doctrine is, that each mental faculty is exercised by means of a portion of the brain, called its organ, the size and quality of which determine its power. It embodies the only true SCIENCE OF MIND and philosophy of human nature ever divulged. It analyzes all the human elements and functions, thereby showing of what materials we are composed, and how to develop them.

PHRENOLOGY shows how the bodily conditions influence mind and morals—a most eventful range of truth. It teaches the true system of Education, shows how to classify pupils, to develop and discipline each faculty separately, and all collectively, into as perfect beings as our hereditary faults will allow. Indeed, to Phrenology and Physiology mainly is the world indebted for its modern educational improvements, and most of its leaders in this department are phrenologists.

PHRENOLOGY teaches parents for what occupation in life their children are best adapted, and in which they can, and can not, be successful and happy. It also teaches parents the exact characteristics of children, and thereby how to manage and govern them properly; to what motives or faculties to appeal, and what to avoid, what desires to restrain, and what to call into action, etc.

PHRENOLOGY and PHYSIOGNOMY teach us our fellow-men; disclose their real character; tell us whom to trust and mistrust, whom to select and reject for specific places and stations; enable mechanics to choose apprentices who have a particular knack or talent for particular trades; show us who will, and will not, make us warm and perpetual friends, and who are, and are not, adapted to become partners in business. More, they even decide, beforehand, who can, and who can not, live together affectionately and happily in wedlock, and on what points differences will be most likely to arise.

Most of all, PHRENOLOGY and PHYSIOLOGY teach us OUR OWN SELVES; our faults, and how to obviate them; our excellences, and how to make the most of them; our proclivities to virtue and vice, and how to nurture the former and avoid provocation to the latter.

TESTIMONIALS.

If the opinions of learned and eminent professional men, both in Europe and America, in regard to the truth and utility of Phrenology be of any account, then the following testimonials should have some weight with unbiased readers.

Let man confine himself to the phenomena of nature, regardless of the dogmas of metaphysical subtilty; let him utterly abandon speculative supposition for positive facts, and he will then be able to apprehend the mysteries of organization. —DR. GALL.

While I was unacquainted with the facts on which it is founded, I scoffed, with many others, at the pretensions of the new philosophy of mind as promulgated by Dr. Gall. Having been disgusted with the uselessness of what I had listened to in the University of Edinburgh (on mental science), I became a zealous student of what I now conceive to be the truth. During the last twenty years I have lent my aid in resisting a torrent of ridicule and abuse, and have lived to see the true philosophy of mind establishing itself wherever talent is found capable of estimating its immense value.—SIR G. S. MACKENZIE, *President of the Royal Society, Edinburgh.*

For more than thirteen years I have paid some attention to Phrenology, and I beg to state, the more deeply I investigate it, the more I am convinced of the truth of the science. I have examined it in connection with the anatomy of the brain, and find it beautifully to harmonize. I have tested the truth of it on numerous individuals, whose characters it unfolded with accuracy and precision. For the last ten years I have taught Phrenology publicly, in connection with Anatomy and Physiology, and have no hesitation in stating that, in my opinion, it is a science founded on truth, and capable of being applied to many practical and useful purposes.—ROBERT HUNTER, M.D., *Professor of Anatomy, University, Glasgow.*

I have great pleasure in stating my firm belief in the truth and great practical utility of Phrenology. This belief is the result of the most thorough investigation, and was proved by evidence that to my mind seemed almost, if not altogether irresistible.—JAMES SHANNON, *President of Bacon College, Ky., Prof. Mental and Moral Science.*

As far as twelve years' observation and study entitle me to form any judgment, I not only consider Phrenology the true science of mind, but also as the only one that, with a sure success, may be applied to the education of children and to the treatment of the insane and criminals. C. OTTO, M.D., *Professor of Medicine in the University of Copenhagen.*

I candidly confess that until I became acquainted with Phrenology, I had no solid foundation upon which I could base my treatment for the cure of insanity.—SIR WILLIAM ELLES, M.D., *Physician to the Lunatic Asylum, Middlesex, England.*

All moral and religious objections against the doctrines of Phrenology are utterly futile.—ARCHBISHOP WHATELY.

As an artist, I have at all times found Phrenology advantageous in the practice of my art; and that *expression, in almost every case, coincided* exactly with what was indicated by the cerebral development.—GEORGE RENNIE, ESQ., *Sculptor.*

I have long been acquainted with the science of Phrenology, and feel no hesitation in declaring my conviction of its truth. In Phrenology we find the best exposition of the moral sentiments, and the most approved metaphysical doctrines heretofore taught, while it surpasses all former systems in practical utility and accordance with facts; being that *alone* which is adequate to explain the phenomena of mind. This opinion, I am emboldened to pronounce, not merely as my own conviction, but as that which I have heard expressed by some of the most scientific men and best logicians of the day.—RICH.

D. EVANSON, M.D., *Prof. Practice of Physiology, R. C. S., Dublin, Ireland.*

No sooner had I read Dr. Gall's work, than I found I had made the acquaintance of one of those extraordinary men whom dark envy is always eager to exclude from the rank to which their genius calls, and against whom it employs the arms of cowardice and hypocrisy. High cerebral capacity, profound penetration, good sense, varied information, were the qualities which struck me as distinguishing Gall. The indifference which I first entertained for his writings gave place to the most profound veneration. Phrenology is true. The mental faculties of men may be appreciated by an examination of their heads.—JOSEPH VIMONT, M.D., *of Paris, an eminent Physician and Author.*

I declare myself a hundred times more indebted to Phrenology than to all the metaphysical works I ever read. * * Mental Philosophy is a Natural Science. The human mind is the most important part of nature. It rests on experience, observation, and induction. It is a science of facts, phenomena, and laws. * * * This science of mind is neglected because its benefits are not immediately apparent; its attainments are not capable of display. * * The phrenological division of faculties of the mind is far more numerous than any other; it looks to the classes of actions or functions mind has to perform, and finds faculties to perform them, as the naturalist, who could not find the ear of a fish by looking externally, looked from the lobe in the brain where the auditory nerve should terminate outwardly, and found it. * * * I look upon Phrenology as the guide to philosophy and the handmaid of Christianity. Whoever disseminates true Phrenology is a public benefactor.—HORACE MANN.

We deem it right to mention that Phrenology appears to us to be true, in as far as it assigns a natural basis to the mind, and that it is entitled to a very respectful attention for the support given to it by a vast amount of careful observation, and the strikingly enlightened and philanthropic aims for which many of its supporters have been remarkable.—JOHN CHAMBERS, *of Chambers' Edinburgh Journal.*

The more I study nature, the more am I satisfied with the soundness of phrenological doctrines.—J. MACKINTOSH, M.A.

By this science the faculties of the mind have been, for the first time, traced to their elementary forms.—ROBERT CHAMBERS, *of Chambers' Journal.*

Phrenology has added a new and verdant field to the domain of human intellect.—REV. THOS. CHALMERS, D.D.

Phrenology undertakes to accomplish for man what Philosophy performs for the external world—it claims to disclose the real state of things, and to present nature unvailed and in her true feature.—PROF. BENJ. SILLIMAN.

To a phrenologist the Bible seems to open up its broadest and highest beauties.—REV. P. W. DREW.

Phrenology is the true Science of Mind. Every other system is defective in enumerating, classifying, and tracing the relations of the faculties.—PROF. R. H. HUNTER.

If we would know the truth of ourselves, we must interrogate Phrenology, and follow out her teachings, as we would a course of religious training, after we had once became satisfied of its truth. * * * The result of all my experience for something over two-score years is this: that Phrenology is a revelation put by God himself within the reach of all His intelligent creation to be studied and applied in all the relations and in all the business of life; that we are all of us both phrenologists and physiognomists in spite of ourselves, and without knowing it, and that we have only to enlarge our observations, and be honest and true to ourselves, and these two sciences will have no terrors for us, and our knowledge of them, instead of being hurtful or mischievous, would only serve to make us wiser and better, and therefore happier, both here and hereafter; and in conclusion, let me say that I have never yet examined a sturdy disbeliever with a head worth having.—HON. JOHN NEAL.

All my life long I have been in the habit of using Phrenology as that which solves the practical phenomena of life. Not that I regard the system as a completed one, but that I regard it as far more useful and far more practical and sensible than any other system of mental philosophy which has yet been evolved. Certainly, Phrenology has introduced mental philosophy to the common people. Hitherto, mental philosophy has been the business of philosophers and metaphysicians—and it has just been about as much business as they needed for their whole lives; but since the day of Phrenology, its nomenclature, its simple and sensible division of the human mind, and its mode of analyzing it, the human mind has been brought within reach and comprehension of ordinary common intelligent people. And now, all through the reading part of our land, it may be said that Phrenology is so far diffused that it has become the philosophy of the common people. The learned professions may do what they please, the common people will try these questions, and will carry the day, to say nothing of the fact that all great material and scientific classes, though they do not concede the truth of Phrenology, are yet digesting it, and making it an integral part of the scientific system of mental philosophy.—REV. HENRY WARD BEECHER.

I speak literally, and in sincerity, when I say, that were I at this moment offered the wealth of India on condition of Phrenology being blotted from my mind forever, I would scorn the gift; nay, were everything I possessed in the world placed in one hand and Phrenology in the other, and orders issued for me to choose one, Phrenology, without a moment's hesitation, would be preferred.—GEORGE COMBE, *Author " Constitution of Man."*

We may also mention the names of the following prominent men who have accepted Phrenology as a true science, and in various ways given it the support of their influence:

Dr. JOHN W. FRANCIS.	Prof. S. G. MORTON.	Hon. HORACE GREELEY
Dr. CHARLES A. LEE.	Prof. S. G. HOWE.	WM. C. BRYANT.
Dr. J. V. C. SMITH.	Prof. GEO. BUSH.	Hon. AMOS DEANE.
Dr. MCCLINTOCK.	Judge E. P. HURLBUT.	Rev. ORVILLE DEWEY.
Dr. JOHN BELL.	Hon. T. J. RUSK.	Rev. JOHN PIERPONT.
Prof. C. CALDWELL.	Hon. WM. H. SEWARD.	Hon. S. S. RANDALL.

Phrenology being true, it should be learned, and cordially embraced by all, and its benefits appropriated. It comes to mankind, not as a partisan or sectarian proposition, but as the voice of God revealed in nature to aid and guide mankind.

Phrenological Journal Office, 389 Broadway, New York.

THE UTILITY OF PHRENOLOGY.

"I look upon Phrenology as the guide to philosophy and the handmaid of Christianity."—HORACE MANN.

To one unacquainted with the nature of Phrenology this may seem an exalted assumption. The experienced philanthropist and educator, however, knew well of what he was speaking, and his earnest tribute is warranted by facts. The science we advocate is regenerative and beneficent. It is a great good to man, individually and socially. To be specific, we will state some of the particulars in which Phrenology is useful.

It is useful because it presents the only sure basis upon which character and disposition may be interpreted, errors pointed out, and methods of reformation prescribed.

It is useful because practical in its adaptations. It considers the human organization as it exists; where there is a lack of harmony it indicates the source of that lack, and the means of improvement by employing counteracting influences, already in the organization, which have been neglected.

It enables the parent to understand the natural characteristics of her child, and to intelligently unfold its budding mind.

It enables the teacher to analyze the temperaments and cerebral capacities of his pupils, and properly classify them, and so to adapt his instruction that they shall make the best progress commensurate with their several abilities.

Its utility is further seen in the assistance it renders to young men who would select pursuits in life best suited to their natural capabilities; relieving them of uncertainty and hesitation with respect to this important subject, and giving them assurance of ultimate success.

Phrenology is of great importance to the merchant or manufacturer, or any who require skillful and intelligent aid in the prosecution of enterprises. It enables them to select with confidence those persons whose service will prove of the greatest advantage, and thus obviate the disappointment and embarrassment resulting from incompetent help.

It enables the business man to understand his customers, and to conduct his negociations more satisfactorily and successfully.

Instructed by those " signs of character " which science has classified he can avoid the fraudulent and disagreeable, and consort only with the just, honorable and the kindly.

In social life, as in the individual character, Phrenology exerts a beneficent and reformatory influence. They who know each other best can best associate, and their mutual influence will be mutually improving.

Applied to politics, Phrenology would operate as a check upon partizanship, and promote the welfare of communities by the elevation of honest and capable men to positions of trust. Intelligent men, however strongly imbued by party feelings, are not likely to sanction the election to an office of a candidate whom they know to be altogether incapable of discharging its duties. They would have their public servants competent to meet the requisitions of office, because their own personal interests are concerned ; and they would advance those interests not depreciate them.

Phrenology furnishes correct data by which those who have the care of the insane and vicious in hospitals and in prisons, may be guided, and confidently expect good results.

In general society the use of Phrenology tends to inspire closer intimacy, cordial sympathy, and a more liberal spirit. The rough and disagreeable man knowing his disposition to be thoroughly understood by others would endeavor to modify it, and so gradually become gentle and courteous. The pompous and domineering man, finding little encouragement for his peculiar characteristics among those whose good opinion he would have, would seek to check his loftiness and cultivate the spirit of conformity ; while the diffident and weak would find encouragement and gain confidence and self-reliance.

By the adaptation of Phrenological principles to his avocation the clergyman would be enabled to do his onerous duties better, and the benevolent man would be instructed in dispensing his bounty. We fully indorse the statement, that, " Whoever disseminates true Phrenology is a public benefactor."

It is the office of the PHRENOLOGICAL JOURNAL AND LIFE ILLUSTRATED, a first-class Magazine, to both teach and apply Phrenology. The Prospectus, to which we refer the reader, sets forth in a detailed manner its special mission.

THE PHRENOLOGICAL JOURNAL & LIFE ILLUSTRATED,

is a First Class Family Magazine, devoted to the SCIENCE OF MAN, including Phrenology, Physiology, Physiognomy, Psychology, Ethnology, Natural History, etc. It is the only Journal of the kind in America, or, indeed, in the world. . It is edited by S. R. WELLS, Author of New Physiognomy. Terms only $3 a year in advance. Sample numbers, 30 cts.

A LIST OF NEW PREMIUMS FOR 1869.

In addition to a monthly magazine, which is richly worth its price, we now offer to those who may send us new subscriptions, valuable premiums. As this JOURNAL is essentially useful and substantial in its general character, so the premiums named are of a useful and substantial sort. We offer no worthless frippery—no mean "pinchbeck ware" or "sham jewelry." As regards the liberal terms we make in this "premium business," we invite comparison with the best inducements offered by other magazines. They are worth working for

CHOICE PREMIUMS. CASH VALUE. NO. OF SUBSCRIBERS.

Names of Articles.	Cash Value.	No. Sub's. at $3 ea.	Names of Articles.	Cash value.	No. Sub's. at $3 ea.
1. Piano, Steinway or Weber, 7 octave	$450	350	16. Rosewood Writing Desk, furnished	12	9
2. Organ, Mason & Hamlin or Berry, 5 octave	170	100	17. Webster's Illust'd Quarto Dictionary	12	9
3. Choice Library, your selection	140	70	18. Irving's Life of Washington, 5 vols	12 50	8
4. Metropolitan Organ, M. & H., 5 octave	130	60	19. Mitchell's General Atlas, folio	10	8
5. Gold Hunting Watch, American Co.'s best	125	60	20. Student's Set of Phrenological Works	10	7
6. Choice Library, your selection	75	50	21. Universal Clothes Wringer	9	7
7. Chambers' Encyclopedia, new, 10 vols	45	30	22. " Bruen Cloth Plate," for Sewing Machines	10	6
8. Silver Hunting Watch, American best	60	30	23. Stereoscope, Rosewood, 12 fine views	7	6
9. Sewing Machine, Wood's new style	60	25	24. New Physiognomy, Illustrated	5	4
10. Sewing Machine, Wheeler and Wilson's	55	20	25. Weaver's Works, in one vol	3	3
11. Chest of Tools, 25 pieces	40	25	26. Hand-Book—How to Write, Talk, Behave,		
12. Library, your choice	30	20	and Do Business. In one vol.	2 25	2
13. Lange's Commentaries, any 3 vols	15	10	27. Life in the West, new	2	2
14. Doty's Washing Machine	$14	10	28. New American Gazetteer of the World	10	8
15. Irving's "Belles Lettres Works," 8 vols	14	9	29. Appleton's New American Encyclopedia,	80	40

Two old subscribers will be counted as *one* new subscriber, and the premiums awarded accordingly. Our own books may be substituted in all cases for any other premium if preferred.

The articles enumerated are the best of their several kinds. The "Belles Lettres" set of Irving comprises "Knickerbocker," "Tales of a Traveller," "Wolfert's Roost," "Crayon Miscellany," "Bracebridge Hall," "Alhambra," "Oliver Goldsmith," and "Sketch Book."

It is scarcely necessary to say that the pianos and parlor organs on our list are acknowledged among the best manufactured in the world.

The Mason and Hamlin cabinet organ offered as premium No. 2 is a five octave double reed instrument with four stops, having their new and very valuable improvements introduced this season, viz. "Mason & Hamlin's Improved Vox Humana," and "Monroe's Improved Reeds."

All know what the Sewing Machines are. We have sent out many of the Wheeler and Wilson which have, of course, given the best of satisfaction.

The Bruen Cloth Plate, is a valuable contrivance, and when attached to the Wheeler and Wilson Machine, makes the Grover and Baker stitch, a desideratum in Embroidery by machine. EVERY WOMAN WANTS IT.

It is believed, that a little energy, enterprise, and well directed effort, will enable some one in every town and neighborhood, to secure a Club of subscribers, for the JOURNAL, and more or less of these premiums.

REMITTANCES should be made in post-office orders, bank checks, or drafts payable to the order of S. R. WELLS, 389 Broadway, New York.

PHRENOLOGICAL JOURNAL AND LIFE ILLUSTRATED.

The Phrenological Journal and Life Illustrated, is a handsome monthly, devoted to the Science of Man, including Phrenology, Physiology, Physiognomy, Psychology, Ethnology, Sociology, etc. It is the only Journal of the kind in America, or, indeed, in the world. Terms only $3 a year in advance. Samples numbers, 30 cts. Address, SAMUEL R. WELLS, 389 Broadway, New York.

NOTICES OF THE PRESS.

Few books will better repay perusal in the family than this rich storehouse of instruction and entertainment, which never fails to illustrate the practical philosophy of life with its lively expositions, appropriate anecdotes, and agreeable sketches of distinguished individuals.—*New York Tribune.*

It is not necessary, we trust, to accept the doctrines of Phrenology in all their fullness, in order to enjoy the Phrenological Journal. Perhaps no publication in the country is guided by clearer common sense or more self-reliant independence. Certainly none seems better designed to promote the health, happiness, and usefulness of its readers; and although we cannot imagine a person who could read a number of it without dissent from some of its opinions, we should be equally at a loss to fancy one who could do so without pleasure and profit.—*Round Table.*

It grows steadily in variety and value. It is not confined to discussions of Phrenology, but deals with all questions affecting the good of society.—*Evening Post.*

It takes us longer to read the Phrenological Journal and Life Illustrated, than any other periodical which comes to our office. Its articles are various and interesting, and beneficial to the intellect and morality of the readers.—*Religious Herald, Hartford.*

Besides the matter pertaining to its speciality, the Phrenological Journal contains a great variety of articles that will interest many readers.—*Christian Intelligencer.*

One of the pleasantest and most readable papers that comes to our office. It is always filled with interesting valuable matter.—*New York Chronicle.*

A periodical which, more, perhaps, than any other publication in the world, is calculated to do good to its readers—to promote their physical, moral and intellectual health—to point out the dangers and temptations of life, and indicate the remedy for any evils that may have already been entailed. Alive, progressive, shrewd, practical, fully up to, if not in advance of the times in every respect, this monthly is working incalculable good, exerting its influence even upon those unaware of its existence. It ought to have a place in every family, and once having gained a foothold, its maintenance of it is sure.—*Trenton Monitor.*

Its practical teachings are of the highest value in the promotion of physical development and health, and *all aim* at moral improvements.—*The Methodist.*

Indispensable to believers in the science, and valuable and illustrative to the general reader. It is edited with marked ability, and beautifully printed.—*Chris. Inq.*

We find both instruction and amusement in this monthly visitor.—*Chris. Advocate.*

There are few periodicals more truly valuable as household companions than this publication. We always find it readable throughout, and always up to a high standard of instructive family literature. The specialities are health and education, and on these topics its editorials and selections are unrivalled.—*Wheeling Intelligencer.*

The Phrenological Journal is a live, wide-awake, and progressive institution. Its talk about Physiognomy, Ethnology, Phrenology, Physiology, etc., is both interesting and instructive, and its numerous illustrations add to the beauty and value of the magazine. It is the standard in its sphere of journalism, and deservedly popular all over the land.—*Moore's Rural New Yorker.*

The Phrenological Journal has portraits and biographical sketches of prominent persons, both of this and foreign countries. It is a magazine conveying knowledge that cannot easily be obtained from any other source.—*Providence (R. I.) Evening Press.*

The Phrenological Journal should be in the hands of every one interested in the study of human character.—*Rock Island Daily Union.*

No other journal in America imparts in one year so much valuable information as does this, and certainly no other teaches man so well to know himself. Each single number is worth the entire amount of a year's subscription.—*Cumberland (Md.) Telegraph.*

The Phrenological Journal and Life Illustrated is one of the most pleasant periodicals published. It contains an amount of reading matter far more sensible and instructive than can be found in many journals of greater pretensions. Even those who disapprove of the science of Phrenology as taught, can not fail to perceive the high tone of the paper. Its articles show careful selections.—*National Union, South Bend, Ind.*

This scientific monthly is one of the most useful and beneficial works issued from the American press. It should be read by every family in our country.—*Mystic Star.*

LIFE IS ILLUSTRATED IN ALL ITS

various phases in the PHRENOLOGICAL JOURNAL—a First-class Monthly Magazine—now in its *Forty-eighth Volume*, edited and published in the city of New York, at $3 a year, by S. R. WELLS, at 389 Broadway.

SPECIAL OBJECTS OF THE JOURNAL.

Anthropology; or, the Science of Man, considered PHYSICALLY, INTELLECTUALLY, and SPIRITUALLY, forms a leading feature in the JOURNAL.

Phrenology—the Brain and its Functions; the location of the different groups—social, selfish, perceptive, reflective, moral—and their respective organs, with the office or function of each, is given, with directions How to Cultivate the Memory, and to improve the mind.

Physiology—the Temperaments; Dietetics; Exercise; Bodily Growth; Hours of Study and Sleep; Laws of Life, with How to Secure and Retain "Health at Home," on Hygienic principles.

Physiognomy; or, the Science of Expression" in the Human Face, Voice, Walk, Action, with other Signs of Character, and "How to Read Them." If one may *sometimes* detect a rogue or an impostor *without* the rules of science, he can do so much more *certainly* with reliable rules, such as are taught in this JOURNAL.

Psychology; or, "the Science of the Soul." The Immortal part, in relation to the Here and the Hereafter, may be better understood and appreciated when looked at from our stand-point. We propose to give the History of All Religious Sects and Creeds, in connection with man's spiritual state, growth in grace, change of heart, the better life, etc.

"What to Do." The question "What Can I Do Best?" occurs to every one, and the choice of a life pursuit is the most important step in every man's history. Success or failure; riches or poverty; fame or infamy; happiness or misery, depend on the choice of a calling, or the occupation in which a person engages. One may shine in the law, another in medicine, another in divinity; one is inventive; another prefers agriculture, commerce, mechanism, or manufacturing. Phrenology "puts the right man in the right place."

Marriage. "Be ye not unequally yoked." Temperament indicates who are and who are not adapted to each other in this relation. Phrenology discloses the natural disposition of each, enabling the parties to know in advance what to expect, and how to conform where differences exist. Why not consult it?

Children. The right education and proper training of children is *vastly important*. The usual methods are faulty. Lives are often sacrificed by too close confinement to books and to brain work. Children should be *classified* by teachers according to temperament, constitution, and capacity. They should be *governed* according to organization and disposition. Our science affords the only means by which to arrive at correct conclusions concerning temperament, disposition, character, tendency, and innate capability.

The Criminal, the Insane, the Imbecile, the Idiotic, the Inebriate, the Pauper, and the Vagrant should be classified, employed, trained, educated, and developed according to their several characters. *All may be improved;* some, made self-supporting. Phrenology and Physiology should be understood and applied by those having charge of these classes.

Finally. Our public men, servants of trust, our preachers and our teachers, ought to be chosen or selected with reference to their constitutional fitness for the several posts to be filled. Neglect of this important principle gets communities into quarrels, contentions, confusion. Ignorance and corruption combine to put thieves in places of trust. We have perverted and dissipated gamblers and pot-house politicians where we should have statesmen. A thorough knowledge of Phrenology would serve to correct these evils. To disseminate such knowledge is one of the objects of THE PHRENOLOGICAL JOURNAL. Our writers are among the foremost in science, philosophy, literature, art, and education. The editor rides no hobby; is tied to no ism, ology, or party. MAN is his theme; the world is his field, and with God for his guide, he will work for the improvement and elevation of the one, and the approval of the other.

READER, this is our programme. Are you with us? The best field in which to work is at home; lend your JOURNALS; indoctrinate your neighbors. Begin at once, and may God abundantly bless with large accessions all good efforts in behalf of human improvement and human happiness!

H117 80 11

www.ingramcontent.com/pod-product-compliance
Lightning Source LLC
Chambersburg PA
CBHW020028030726
47499CB00007B/2326